The Christmas Squirrel

The Christmas Squirrel

(Miracle of the Silver Bell)

by

Elmer Garten

Copyright © Elmer Garten
All rights reserved.
ISBN: 9798351923253 (HBK)
   9798849634098 (PPB)

For the Nice
And
The Naughty.

I admire the first
And grateful for the second.

I cannot thank Miz Mari enough for all the patience, consideration and encouragement she has given me during the creation of this little book. I don't believe for a moment I could have possibly completed it without her help. In other words, what you are about to read is entirely her fault.

Content

Chapter 1:
What Child is This 11

Chapter 2:
Dashing Through The Snow...................**20**

Chapter 3:
A Merry Little Crisis **30**

Chapter 4:
The Bottom Copy **43**

Chapter 5:
Golden Rings **52**

Chapter 6:
A Foggy Christmas Eve **61**

Chapter 7:
Perspectives **64**

Chapter 8:
All That and a Can of Popcorn...............**75**

Chapter 9:
From Your Lips to God's Ear **95**

Chapter 10:
Game Theory **110**

Chapter 11:
Always Bring The Whip **113**

Chapter 12:
When One Door Closes..........................**121**

Chapter 13:
The Upside of Zero **128**

Chapter 14:
The Downside of Zero 136

Chapter 15:
The Suppository of All Knowledge 141

Chapter 16:
A Fistful of Collar....................................152

Chapter 17:
Santa's Big Day 169

Chapter 18:
A Turkey and Some Mistletoe 174

Chapter 19:
Don't You Tell A Single Soul 188

Chapter 20:
Everybody Believes in Somebody..........196

Chapter 21:
The Happy Dog..211

Chapter 22:
The Bell Curve...226

Chapter 23:
Nor Doth He Sleep 229

Chapter 24:
The Cards on the Table 238

Chapter 25:
Every One 240

Chapter 1:

What Child is This

Candice Siwel was a Nubian Princess. At least that's what her mother told her. Her earliest recollection was both of them living on the back seat of Hyatt's old car. The seat was a beige vinyl bordered by faded maroon trim piping and a few unraveled seams. Hyatt himself was a greasy haired white man with a bad complexion and yellow black teeth. He always wore a wrinkled bowling shirt, perspired profusely and smelled horrible like gym shoes burning in a backed up port-a-potty. Bad enough the whole car wreaked of him but he slobbered his stink all over her mother who laid there because she had to as he grunted, panted, wheezed and drooled his way to self-gratification —every night.

Hyatt did not appreciate the Nubian Princess either. She had to remain very quiet. He lashed out at Candice over the tiniest noises. Her mother would push herself between them and take the brunt of his rage but it still hurt something awful. So Candy, that's what her mother loved to call little Candice, stifled her laughs, squeals and cries to a tiny little squeak —about all Hyatt could condone. She never, never, never picked at the maroon trim either. Her mother taught her that. When she had to ask for something, she would only whisper softly into her mother's ear. Candy confined most of her playing to the inside of her head. If she got too rambunctious, that is to say moved around a little, it would pique Hyatt and he would beat them both severely. So Candy learned to just stare at a toy and imagine wonderful games and adventures right there in her mind where Hyatt wouldn't be bothered.

That's how they lived until Hyatt found someone he liked better than her mother. Then he threw them both out of the car. Candy remembered that day. It was cold and icy. Snow and wind stung her face, nose and ears. Red blood from her mother's lip dripped on the white snow covered ground where they sat shivering as Hyatt drove away. Her mother wrapped her arms around little Candice and said not to worry. They wouldn't die. They didn't.

They spent most of that winter on the street. Her mother foraged food from the garbage bins of restaurants. Fast food was the best. Children only pick at their meal in a restaurant so they made the most leftovers. In Fast Food places, each item would be thrown out still wrapped in its original paper. Approaching pristine, often only one or two bites gone. In a regular restaurant, separate dishes would be scraped into one pile before being tossed out. Always yucky. Her mother told Candy it wouldn't taste so bad if they prayed over it first. So Candy was sure the regular restaurant food must have really tasted terrible to start out with. Because no matter how much they prayed, it was very bad.

When they could find an unlocked public restroom, they would clean up. They went early in the morning before the druggies were out. Her mother taught her that. Public Libraries were the best places. Truck stops if the cashier was sympathetic. Gas stations were the worst, but you get what you get when you get it and should always be thankful for what you get. Her mother taught her that.

The hardest thing to find was a safe, warm place to sleep. Alleys were okay if they weren't facing the wind and the people in them were friendly. Underpasses and tunnels much better but always crowded. Park benches smelled best but were open, cold and dangerous. Homeless shelters were the deadliest of all. The monsters of the city would comb those places for victims and the onsite administrators offered little or no protection. Candy and her mother preferred stairwells as did everybody. An empty building stairwell accessible after hours was a godsend. Her mother taught her that. It was in one of those stairwells they met Fen.

Fenimore Mulligan lived in a tiny single room apartment on the fourth floor of a five story building. He was very old, very fat and very lonely. He was divorced and widowed with two estranged children who never visited or called him. It didn't take much for her mother to charm Fen and less for Fen to lure her mother into his home.

It was nice living with Mulligan. Her mother cleaned, cooked and shopped for him. In turn, Fen gave her mother a nice allowance and never slobbered on the woman. Not even once. He just watched her mother. She was, after all, a beautiful woman as one might expect the mother of a Nubian Princess to be.

Fen didn't get mad when her mother used his money to buy Candy new dresses to start school. He seemed absolutely delighted and as excited as her mother. He even had Candy model them for him and her mother. The one Candy liked best, he liked as well and commended Candy for her excellent taste in clothes. Candy wanted a little purse to complete her ensemble so Fen asked her mother to get one. He insisted in fact and her mother did. Candy would always keep that purse.

One day, Candy came home with tears flowing down her cheeks. Children had teased her for explaining how she was a Nubian Princess. Mulligan didn't scold Candy for her single mournful squeak.

He was very sympathetic. He hugged her and wiped her tears but told her he wasn't at all surprised. Most people were just too stupid to know a beautiful Nubian Princess when they saw one and wouldn't know how to treat one anyway. The best thing Candy could do for those poor unfortunate morons was not even broach the subject. Let it pass. All the best and brightest people in the world would recognize her immediately and treat her accordingly though they would probably be too polite to bring it up either.

Fen suggested Candy listen and learn all the biggest, longest words she could. "Everybody respects a person who knows how to use really big words," Fenimore told her. The first step in becoming the richest, most respected person on the planet is knowing the most big words. "That's how lawyers do it," Fen said. So Candy made it a point to memorize any impressive sounding word she heard and practice using it. To her astonishment, Fen was absolutely right. Whenever Candy would use one of her big words, most bullies became dumbfounded, stared blankly, mouths agape and afterwards leave her alone. Sometimes, they out and out ran from her. But alas, there were only so many big words floating around in Candy's world so she started minting her own.

Then Fenimore Mulligan died. His estranged children showed up, seized his bank accounts and had Candy and her mother evicted right before Christmas. They were again homeless. And it was again snowing and cold. It was a little after New Year's when people put their old Christmas trees on the street that Candy's mother became very sick.

They were sheltering at the bottom of another stairwell in another old apartment building when her mother told her she was probably going to Heaven soon and couldn't bring Candy along. Candy cried. It was a very soft squeak, maybe two, of sorrow but the tears flowed inexorably. That was when her mother gave her a little plastic Silver Bell ornament and asked Candy to always keep it in her purse. The ornament looked just like several others they had seen earlier on a tinsel covered Christmas tree tossed out for trash pickup. But her mother assured her this one was special and whispered in Candy's ear why.

Candy put the little ornament in her purse and laid there in her mother's arms all night. The next morning, Candy's mother was dead. When the men came, it was clear to Candy why she couldn't go to Heaven with her mother. Apparently, they zip you up in a bag and haul you away in a big van for that.

Little Candice Siwel became a ward of the state. She spent the rest of her childhood bouncing between foster homes and the orphanage. After her twelfth Birthday, Candy spent most of her time in a privately funded dormitory for homeless and wayward children. She was only invited into personal homes for the holidays.

Most of the families that agreed to take her during the holidays never asked her back. No one knew why. It could have been her being abnormally quiet. A single mouselike squeak instead of laughing or crying or any of the noises most children make. Whispering instead of shouting. Or her playing with toys in her head rather than out in the open for all the world to see. Or her use of freshly minted big words. Or maybe Fenimore Mulligan was right. Most folks were just too stupid to know a Nubian Princess when they saw one.

Whatever the reason, Candice Siwel was about to age out of the orphanage system. Soon Candy would have no place to stay, no place to turn and no place to go. She would be homeless, penniless and alone. Even worse, it looked like snow.

Chapter 2:

Dashing Through The Snow

Skeptics say there is no such thing as a miracle, let alone a Christmas Miracle. However, there are three irrefutable events that occur every Christmas Eve somewhere in America that, when they occur together, prove exactly the opposite. It is just that these events occur on the biggest holiday of the year and most skeptics are too drunk to notice. Those three events are: Inclement Weather, Last Minute Shopping and The Office Party.

1) Inclement Weather. Snow is made of ice. That is an immutable fact. It is also a fact that, at the first sign of snow, folks hurry to reach their various destinations before the snow turns to ice. That is a fallacy. Snow is not going to turn to ice. It already is ice. Any time snow begins to fall is not a

good time to be driving anywhere at all, let alone anywhere fast. Still people always do.

2) Last Minute Shopping. Most women, particularly wives and mothers, have finished all their Christmas shopping by Christmas Eve. Most men, particularly husbands and boy friends, are just starting theirs. To be fair, the smart ones started the day before. That's a problem. Most shops, except a few selling jewelry and lingerie, close early on Christmas Eve. Of course, there is always that random appliance store still open for the callow husband to get something unforgettable for that wife who has everything —except a divorce. Nonetheless, most places are closed or closing when most men and boys are racing from store to store desperately hunting for that perfect something for their perfect someone that will guarantee their perfect relationship will live another day. Fortunately for all of them, women have a very forgiving and understanding nature.

3) The Office Party. Very little actual work gets done in the offices, studios and cubicles of corporate America on Christmas Eve. Secret Santas, gag

gifts and employee raffles cap a day of laughter, music and inappropriate behavior lubricated with way too much alcohol, most of it in the form of eggnog and rum. By the end of the day, people who should not even be allowed to walk anywhere by themselves stagger out to their cars and drive home.

Any two of these make for a dangerous circumstance. All three and it is a miracle anyone gets home unscathed. Yet most people do without even a dent in their fender. Every Christmas Eve! Truly a Christmas miracle!

That is exactly what happened one particular Christmas Eve. Street lights were trimmed in green tinsel garlands topped with huge silver bells hanging from large red bows. Snow began to fall. Stores began to close. Office parties all over town were winding down, relinquishing their last few drunks into the maelstrom of holiday traffic on icing roads and the last minute shopper rush.

Hamelin Toys was no different. It was a whole sale distribution center and warehouse but, on Christmas Eve, party central for a few hundred office employees. By late afternoon, not half a dozen cars were scattered across its parking lot, the painted lines of the parking spaces already obscured by falling snow. A couple of lone figures, amorphous treasure in one arm and briefcase in the other, could be seen stumbling drunkenly to their respective vehicles. The building itself towered above the parking area like some great squatted rock mesa, all dark except for the frosted pale glow of fluorescent lighting from the upper floors.

On one of those lit floors was an office party wasteland of extinguished Christmas lights, cardboard snowflakes and plastic holly stretched over empty cubicles sprinkled with paper plates, cookie crumbs and overflowing trashcans of wrapping paper and bows. Mistletoe and large plastic silver bells darted the ceiling near doorways and water coolers —little kissing traps for the uninitiated office girl. The whole place smelled of warm eggnog and regurgitated sheet cake.

Dan Oglesby's cubicle was the only one ablaze in under-shelf lighting. That's because Dan Oglesby was the only soul still in his cubicle. He was waiting for his boss.

Dan was a transplant to the midwest with well over twenty-five years invested in his marriage and Hamelin Toys. Originally from Massachusetts, he was a hundred percent Bostonian from his dialect to his love of Fenway Park. He was a total beaner, Hubbub or Masshole, depending on who you asked. He exchanged Rs and Ws liberally and his desk was buried in Red Sox paraphernalia. The only thing Dan loved more than the Red Sox was his family. Which was why he was still waiting for his boss Malynda Piper. He couldn't afford to lose his job. It was also why he was on the phone with his wife Darla. He couldn't afford to lose her either.

Darla Oglesby was not even remotely Bostonian. Not even Eastern Seaboard. She was all Midwest as were her three Daughters. And at the moment, like a lot of other drivers, she was racing down the snowy streets, trying to get home before the snow turned to ice. Skittering through yellow lights, fishtailing over hills and sliding around corners, Darla was completely oblivious to the other drivers trying hard not to hit her. Despite a headset, she was steering with only one hand while holding her cell in the other. Habit, I suppose. Occasionally, she would tap the brake like that made things safer. It did not. She was trying to sound completely agitated with Dan but she wasn't fooling anybody. Darla loved the guy.

"Really, Dan?" Darla said as sarcastically as she could. "What kind of a Scrooge would make you work late on Christmas Eve when I have all this work for you to do at home?

"Funny," Dan replied. "I'm not working. I'm just sitting. It's like she's keeping me after school."

"You didn't say or do anything stupid, Dan?" Darla knew her guy and Dan had a tendency to speak now and think later. Not the best trait.

"I've been a choir boy," Dan said. "Darn it, Darla, I was the only sober guy in the place today."

"It's snowing now, Dan," Darla replied. "You need to start home before the snow turns to ice."

Dan's other line flashed. Malynda Piper's name blazed across his phone display.

"Uh-oh. Got to go," Dan said. "It's the Harpy."

"Well, don't be too late," Darla warned. "Remember, I'm the Queen of the dinner table."

"Love you too." Dan released her line then pressed the flashing one.

"Dan!" Even filtered through a telephone, the voice was as pleasant as nails on a chalk board. "You're still here!"

"You told me to wait."

"I need five more minutes," Malynda had all the aplomb of a cottonmouth approaching a cornered mouse.

"That's what you said thirty minutes ago."

"Unavoidably detained, Dan. Five more." Not one note of sympathy or apology. Just that chalk board screech.

"Okay, Malynda," Dan could say nothing else. "Five more."

Malynda Piper hung up the phone. She was an attractive woman; slender, high cheekbones, auburn hair, deep hazel eyes in an impeccably tailored business suit of midnight blue. Her looks made up for her voice but nothing could make up for the person behind those eyes. Her desk was an honest reflection of her personality —cold, austere and empty. Not a picture nor a plant to be seen. Just a Desk pad. Her back wall, however, was an altar to herself. It was covered in framed diplomas, certifications and awards. Malynda framed and mounted every accreditation she ever got, including perfect attendance awards. Even her first grade report card! There were pictures of her with mucky mucks and industry heads from across the country as well, most of them photo bombs. The rest of her office was so devoid of anything personal that the commemorative souvenir given out to all employees by the company —a little plastic silver bell attached to a tiny candy cane with a red bow —seem to blaze noticeably from the top of her inbox. Malynda wouldn't have noticed though. She was busy calling Ruthie in Payroll.

"Where's that check!" Malynda's tone would have terrified the Wicked Witch of the West.

Ruthie lived in a world of outdated ledgers, rolodexes and adding machines commingled with impact printers and CRT monitors in a closet sized office. The only thing missing were the coat hangers. An untouched slice of cake sat on a paper plate with an unused plastic fork in the least cluttered corner of her desk.

Ruthie rolled her office chair from one pile of work to the other, handset cradled between her shoulder and ear, and pencil clamped firmly between her teeth. The Company's little silver bell souvenir was pinned over her heart. She had been an employee of Hamelin Toys for over thirty-five Year's and a payroll clerk for much longer. She wore frazzled like an old sweater and was quite adept at handling your average wicked witch.

"I'm the only one here, Malynda," she said. "It's Christmas Eve."

"Get it ready, Ruthie." Malynda cracked her tongue like a whip. "I'm coming over."

Malynda stabbed release before Ruthie could answer. She pulled on her coat and grabbed her briefcase to leave when she noticed the little silver bell in her inbox. For just a second, Malynda stared at it thoughtfully then snatched it up and tossed it in the trash. Malynda slapped the light switch on her way out of her office. She liked to slap things.

In the meantime, Ruthie pressed the intercom button to the Executive Office suite where the Hamelin brothers ran the company for longer than most people have been alive. It was Ezra who answered. Saul was busy on his computer.

"Ruthie!" shouted Ezra. "What are you still doing here?"

"Malynda Piper wants an immediate final pay and severance on Dan Oglesby," Ruthie said.

"He's her boy," Ezra replied. "Cut the check then stick around a minute."

Ezra clicked off the intercom and looked at his completely engrossed brother.

"Did you hear what that schmuck you promoted is doing now?" Ezra asked.

Saul didn't even glance up. "You'll have to be more specific, Ezra. They're all schmucks."

Chapter 3:

A Merry Little Crisis

Over at the local precinct, police were disappearing like coins in a magic show. All but a skeleton staff were grabbing packages, pulling on coats, signing out and running for the exits. Vacant desks and the abandoned glass walled cage that served as the Captain's office surrounded a long folding table of empty donut boxes and a very old strand of mostly burned out Christmas tree lights. A coffee pot smoldered on a hot plate beneath a battered honeycomb paper foldout of a silver bell suspended from the ceiling tile by a large mutilated paper clip. Tis the season.

Joe, a uniformed police officer, sat at the duty desk reading *A Visit From Saint Nicholas* over the phone to his kids. The only detective working, that is to say trapped at his desk, was David Caldwell.

Caldwell was the youngest detective at the station, maybe the youngest detective anywhere. A baggy brown suit, finger brushed hair and a gaunt, tired face, he sat there trying not to look disinterested as Johnetta Hoyle, a pompous well-fed socialite of the highest order, rambled on and on about her latest avocation —the capture and arrest of the infamous Pod Pirate. All part of the job. Whenever Johnetta Hoyle walked in, whoever had the least seniority in the room got saddled with her. Today that would be David Caldwell. He was at the end of a double shift and practically out the door when she showed up. All he wanted to do was go home and sleep —maybe through Christmas. He fixed his gaze on her silver bell earrings swaying and bouncing with every word gesticulating out of her. He was just waiting for a pause so he could get a word in.

Finally, Johnetta finished or stalled for lack of air. "I'm telling you, the Pod Pirate is real," she said and there it was. The pause.

"I believe you, Ms. Hoyle," Caldwell replied with all the conviction of a Nihilist. "But then, I just pulled a double shift so I'd pretty much believe anybody."

He drew a breath and lost tempi. Stupid, stupid, stupid. Johnetta retook the floor.

"You can believe he'll do something this Christmas. And you can believe we'll catch him when he does. I've posted a reward." In Johnetta Hoyle's world, people would do almost anything for money.

"That's nice. Reward for who?" In David Caldwell's world, it was hard to follow someone who strung non-sequiturs like pearls on a silk thread —especially at the end of a double shift.

"Mobius Dick, Caldwell." Old Sarge decided to help out his young colleague. The grizzled detective happen to overhear them when he stopped to flip off the hot plate. Sarge found one donut sheltering under an opened box lid on the table. Sarge was good at finding things. He snatched it up and hobbled back to his desk.

"Mobius Dick?" David suddenly knew what Johnetta Hoyle had been bloviating about. "That was a computer virus that didn't do much. Why do you care?"

Johnetta sat up erect and angry. "I chair the Citizen's Action Committee Against the Profane, Offensive and Obscene."

"Caca-poo," Mike, another detective, interjected on his way out the door. Both Caldwell and Ms. Hoyle looked at him. "It's the acronym for Citizen's Action Committee Against blah, blah, blah. CACA-POO," He explained.

Mike was right. The name had been suggested by a smart-aleck college kid when the group was being formed. They adapted the name anyway because Johnetta Hoyle liked it and voted to ignore the acronym. They were the only ones who did.

"Merry Christmas, Mike," David said.

"Find a girl, David!" Mike shouted as he disappeared.

"Mobius Dick inserted one long string of code into school library videos." The young detective shuffled some things around his desk like he might actually have the report. He didn't. "Last year? No. I think maybe five years ago?"

"Spring three years ago," Johnetta replied. "My oh me, you make it sound like nothing."

"Oh no. It was something," Caldwell said. "A little string of code turned a few educational videos into harmless arcade games but it didn't spread or become anything big."

More precisely, Mobius Dick designed a strip of viral code that looped in on itself like a möbius and so was virtually undetectable unless accessed directly. Once inserted into the school library's computer software, it converted educational videos into action games using each video's own graphics. Then one day, a teacher happened to stumble on it and discovered why dozens of little boys were spending all their time in the school library. It wasn't to research school assignments.

"Harmless games?" Johnetta could not believe her ears. "Elves kicking shoemakers, frogs eating Princesses, beans stalking giants, chickens firing nuclear eggs out their tushies…"

"Out their tushies?" Caldwell laughed. It seemed ludicrous. Then again, he had been awake over twenty hours. Everything seemed ludicrous.

"There's nothing funny about violence, Detective Caldwell," Johnetta snipped, "in any of it's forms. Even eggs of war." David laughed again. Too tired. No filters left.

Lugging a stuffed Teddy bear the size of a dinosaur, Detective Riley weaved his way through the open floor plan of the Detective Bureau.

"Another double, Caldwell?" Riley asked as he dragged the toy behemoth over Caldwell's desk papers and across Ms. Hoyle's face, muffling her completely.

"Just finishing, Riley," Caldwell replied calmly, too tired to care about the paper avalanche the toy bear sent flittering from his desk to the floor.

"You really need to find a nice girl," Riley said as he wrangled his plush colossus out the door.

"Merry Christmas, Riley," said Caldwell.

"One more load to go, kid," Riley called back just before the door closed.

The young detective looked over at Johnetta Hoyle, busy un-ruffling and preening after getting scraped by Toyzilla. "You can't catch nobody if there's nobody to catch, Ms. Hoyle."

Caldwell smiled as his eyes wondered down to the desktop disaster left in the wake of Riley's Bearasaurus. He immediately realized his keys were missing and he wasn't getting home without them. Smile gone.

"That virus never showed up anywhere else, Detective Caldwell. Just our school. Whoever did it is local, probably a student."

"We had experts look at that code, Ms. Hoyle." Caldwell was frisking the papers disarrayed across his desk for those keys. "They said none of the teaching staff and certainly none of the students could have designed that thing."

"Somebody did," Ms. Hoyle found herself following the pat down.

"We think some kid brought it to school and uploaded it. It has never showed up again here or anywhere else and it's been, what did you say, five years?"

"Three years, last spring!"

"Hey Caldwell! Doing watch too?" It was Bob, an older detective bundled in a half dozen coats and scarves, sprinting for the door with one large shopping bag of gift wrapped goodies.

"No, Bob," Caldwell answered. "On call every night though."

David was now tossing the spilled papers back on his desk as he tried not very well to surreptitiously search for those keys. Though she had no idea what Caldwell was looking for, Johnetta knew he was looking.

"You need to find a girl, Caldwell," laughed Bob, pausing by the door.

"That's what I told him!" Riley appeared a second time with a second load.

"Hey you got a daughter!" Bob hollered to Riley as he waited for him by the door.

"My daughter is not marrying any cop!" Riley hollered back as he picked his way through the desks Fung-Shwayed across the room. Then to

David, "You do need to find a girl, Caldwell. Just not my girl!"

"Merry Christmas, boys," David was back to staring at the top of his desk. He pulled out the pencil drawer and rifled it, just in case. No keys.

Bob held the door for Riley as he manipulated himself and the packages through.

"Careful with Captain Ahab there!" Bob followed Riley out on a two finger wave.

"You're Captain Ahab?" David Caldwell said to himself in a sudden moment of clarity. Unfortunately, he said it out loud.

"Captain Ahab?" Johnetta parroted. "Wasn't he obsessed with a whale?'

"They don't mean your obsessed, Ms. Hoyle," Caldwell began his obligatory kowtowing. In truth, he was more concerned with his missing keys than Johnetta's impression of him and the department. "They don't mean anything at all. It's kind of a shorthand. He's 'Mobius Dick' so you're 'Captain Ahab'. Like an association is all."

"Captain Ahab!" she hissed. "I could have your job!"

Sarge was finally leaving. Pulling on his parka, he stopped by David's desk in a beneficent show of Christmas spirit.

"Nobody wants his job, Ms. Hoyle," Sarge looked the young detective in the eye as he rescued the car keys from their hiding place beneath the In-Box and placed them in David's hand. "Riley's right, Caldwell," Sarge said. "You need to find yourself a girl; one who can overlook your flaws."

"He's flawed?" Ms. Hoyle hacked.

"He must be. He made detective." Sarge grinned and headed for the door.

David fisted his car keys and smiled relief. "Merry Christmas, Sarge."

Johnetta realized the object of the young man's search. "I can see why you made detective."

The young detective knew now his conversation with the most important person in town would not play well with the Captain, come next week.

Before Caldwell could save what had spiraled into a contentious consult with one decent brown-nosed toadyism, Johnetta Hoyle's BlackBerry erupted. She answered before the second ring while shushing him with her open palm.

"What?!" Johnetta nearly ate her cell. "My oh me, did you try the Novaks?"

The frown stamped indelibly on Johnetta's face suddenly became a patently fake smile as her voice filled with enough honey to choke a Grizzly.

"Say, Detective," Johnetta cooed, "what are you doing this Christmas?"

"A double shift." As tired as he was, Caldwell instinctively knew that was a better answer than sleeping.

Johnetta became immediately disinterested, turned back to her caller as she jumped to her feet and marched for the door.

"Get her things together," she told her cell. "We'll find someone. We have to. It's our last one and we're done with her so we have to do it right."

Caldwell wasn't sure if they were done. He jogged after Johnetta Hoyle as she barreled through the police station to the front exit.

"Are we good, Ms. Hoyle?" David struggled to keep up with her.

"I have to go," she holstered her BlackBerry like a samurai scabbard's a Katana. "Another little crisis."

"Well, have yourself a merry little crisis, I mean Christmas," he stumbled again. He was just too tired for this.

Caldwell barely beat Johnetta to the front door. He intended to hold it open for her. Intend was all he was able to do. She pushed him and the door out of her way in a mad dash for her Jeep Cherokee.

"Don't forget. I've posted a reward," Johnetta called as she took the slippery steps in twos on high heels no less and dove into her ATV. She was seated, buckled in, door closed and engine started. All in one fluid effortless movement. Surprising for a large lady but Ms. Hoyle was a force for even nature to reckon with.

"If you need me, I'm on call the whole holiday," he shouted as her door closed and Johnetta Hoyle's big bucket buggy slid away. It was Caldwell's last ditch effort to ingratiate himself so he wouldn't get such a bad dressing down by the Captain after New Year's. She probably didn't even hear, he thought.

Back inside, Joe at the duty desk put it succinctly. "One crazy lady."

"Not crazy. Driven." Caldwell couldn't help it. Once you're in boot licking mode, it's hard to get the taste out of your mouth.

"Yeah?" Joe replied. "She's gona call you tonight, Caldwell."

David Caldwell nodded and sighed. All he wanted to do was sleep.

"You really should find a nice girl," Joe meant it. Everybody did.

"Merry Christmas, Joe," was all Caldwell said as he headed out the door. It was snowing and an exhausted Detective David Caldwell had to get home before the snow turned to ice.

Chapter 4:

The Bottom Copy

Werner was making his rounds with a large trash bin. He had been picking up after people at Hamelin Toys for almost half a century. In a few short hours, he would have the whole office floor looking like an office floor again —with no overtime! For some, janitor was a job. For Werner, it was a calling.

Watching Werner, Dan Oglesby sat impatiently tapping his pen. Dan was welling up. He didn't know how long it had been but he knew it was more than five minutes. And still no Malynda! He exploded out of his chair, slammed that chair into his desk, jammed his arms into his coat, snapped up his briefcase and stomped to the elevator.

Dan made it all the way to the copier before his anger became bemused sympathy. An office worker bee named Zwang, his slacks and undershorts around his ankles, lay sprawled across the copier, butt down on the scanner plate. Someone had rigged the start button so it would run continuously. A bright light scanned Zwang's exposed posterior every few seconds then a page would shoot out between his legs and over the filled output tray to flutter down to the floor covered with hundreds of copies of his tushy. A big red plastic cup dropped on the floor less than a foot from his dangling fingertips explained it all. Zwang was marinating in Christmas cheer. And this was the end result of his fellow elves.

Zwang was a short, portly old man with a big white fluffy beard. If any employee at Hamelin Toys qualified as Santa Claus, it was him. He had been with the company far longer than Dan or anyone else for that matter, had a ridiculously kind and good natured heart, was a wonderful team player and a forgiving soul. Zwang loved everybody. Unfortunately, that made him the perfect foil for the more insidious among his associates. Most men would get annoyed or angry, eventually. Zwang didn't. Being pants and plopped down on the copier was the inevitable result. He was literally the butt of somebody's joke. And once he sobered up, he would even find it funny. The world needed more people like Zwang. However, the world did not need any more pictures of Zwang's behind.

Dan pulled the tape and paper clip from the start button. The scanner stopped. He shook Zwang's arm. No response. Dan dropped his briefcase and shook Zwang by both shoulders.

"Zwang! Zwang, wake up!" Dan got no response. "Darn it, Zwang! Wake up you big ditz!" he shouted as he shook the sozzled Santa.

Zwang mumbled something, smacked his lips and drifted back off into oblivion.

Dan tried to sit him up but Zwang was completely relaxed, dead weight and gone. After several attempts, Dan pulled up on Zwang's pants. He just couldn't get them over the output tray between Zwang's bent legs. Not even the underpants. Dan stepped back, put his hands on his hips and assessed the situation. He reached behind the copier for the large Out of Service sign and carefully positioned it over Zwang's privates.

Werner and his trash bin were wheeling by. Dan pulled the ream of paper from the output tray and dropped it into the trash bin. He kicked at the pile of moonshots scattered across the floor.

"Don't worry for your friend," said the janitor. "I clean everything."

Relieved of the problem, Dan pulled a twenty from his wallet. The janitor smiled, shook his head and waved it away.

"Is not necessary," Werner said. "It's my job."

Dan pushed the twenty into the Werner's palm and wrapped the janitor's fingers around it. "Merry Christmas, anyway." A big smile on his face, he picked up his briefcase and walked to the elevator. Dan was back in the Christmas spirit.

One floor up in the hallway outside the Hamelin office suite, Malynda was leaving payroll with a large grey envelope. Ruthie was right behind with a purse, lunchbox and another large grey envelope of her own. She artfully juggled all three as she pulled out her keys to lock up.

Malynda wasn't even halfway to the elevator when Ezra poked his head out.

"Malynda!" Ezra called, freezing her in her tracks. "How lucky is this! You're still here!"

Malynda turned slowly. "You want to see me, Ezra?"

"Got a minute?" Ezra was cheerful as ever.

"No."

"Come in anyway," Ezra was not at all vexed by her answer.

Malynda trudged back to the CEO's office.

Ruthie slipped her large, grey envelope to Ezra as she passed him on her way to the elevator.

"Merry Christmas, Ezra," Ruthie said.

"Thank you, Ruthie," Ezra replied looking over the envelope. "You have a nice holiday."

Malynda marched by Ezra through the office door to an uncomfortable looking side chair in front of Saul's desk. She sat down. Saul never looked up from his computer. He stared sternly at the screen through reading glasses precariously balanced on the end of his nose, erratically tapping his keyboard.

Ezra closed the office door and rushed around his desk to his swivel chair.

"How lucky is this, Saul," said Ezra. "Malynda is still here."

"Pisha Paysha, Ezra." Saul's attention was focused on his desktop. "We only need a moment, Malynda."

"I have all the moments you need, Saul," Even openly obsequious, she seemed overbearing.

"How accommodating," said Ezra. "She is so accommodating, Saul."

Ezra slipped his grey envelope into the pencil tray of his desk.

"I can't wait to see her new promo, Ezra," Saul continued tapping away.

"What?" Malynda couldn't mask the abject dread crawling beneath her skin. "I'm a PM now."

"We all wear many hats, Malynda," Saul never looked up once.

"Course you don't have to have it by tomorrow," Ezra said. "Tomorrow's Christmas."

"That would be meshugaas," said Saul. "Tomorrow's Christmas."

"Take until New Year's, if you want," said Ezra.

"A week after, even," said Saul.

Ezra was already rushing around the long desk to Malynda.

"But I don't do campaigns anymore." Malynda protested as Ezra took her elbow and nudged her out of the chair and towards the door.

"You did the last three all by yourself," said Saul.

"I'm a PM now," Malynda sounded like a vulture choking on a frog.

"What's one more," said Ezra, opening the office door.

"See you after New Year's," added Saul without ever making eye contact.

"With the new promo," Ezra said as he pushed Malynda out the door and closed it.

Ezra turned towards his brother. Saul looked up for the first time. Their eyes locked. Saul clamped his lips tightly as Ezra covered his mouth, both stifling laughter.

In the hall, Malynda stood frowning at her grey envelope. An idea flashed through her head. When life gives you lemons, you throw them at somebody. Malynda shoved the envelope into her briefcase and marched to the elevator. She knew what to do.

Except for Christmas lights, tinsel and those silver bell decorations, the Marketing floor looked like a place of business again. Four huge trash bags filled to capacity sat by the elevator. Nearby, Zwang was still peacefully sprawled pants down across the copier but the area looked immaculate. Not a moonshot in sight. Werner was vacuuming.

One of the elevators opened. Malynda marched out and straight to Dan's cubicle. Dan was not there. She turned, slowly sweeping the entire floor with her eyes. Except for the janitor, there was not one sign of life on the whole floor. Malynda pulled her cell phone, flicked through her contacts to Dan's name and punched it.

Dan's car was rumbling over the packed street ice beneath the falling snow when his cell phone started ringing. He fished it from his inside coat pocket and glanced at the display. It showed: "Malynda Piper." He cringed, turned it off and tossed it into the passenger seat.

Back at Hamelin, Malynda's cell ringing was replaced by the message: "We're sorry. The party you called is not available at this time or is out of the coverage area. If you would like to leave a message…"

Malynda hung up and flicked through her contact list. *There's more than one way to throw a lemon.*

Chapter 5:

Golden Rings

The Oglesby house was a two story red brick gingerbread on a street of two story red brick gingerbreads. Outlined in Christmas lights, a wreath of holly on the front door with five foot tall nutcrackers standing guard near a paneled window of Christmas tree glory, it was dressed to the nines for the Holidays —just like all the other houses.

It didn't stop at the door either. Twenty-five years of Christmas keepsakes festooned every inch of every corner in every room in the house except Grampy's overstuffed recliner, the Oglesby official sanctum of Boston Red Sox memorabilia. Grampy Coy was as big a fan as his son and far more Boston. That chair was where Grampy lived with a death grip on his channel changer and Bonanza blaring across the television screen. Everywhere else, it was Christmas.

In the great room, Chasse, the Oglesby's full time housekeeper, culinary expert, child wrangler and family scapegoat set the dining table by flinging place mats, stoneware and cutlery all around like a croupier dealing cards. Speed mattered more than accuracy. Chasse was in a deadlock against the local bus schedule. She almost always ended up taking the late night bus home with the psychos and winos but tonight was Christmas Eve and there would not be a late night bus. If Chasse was going to make it home to her children, she was going to have to leave on time. In the Oglesby household, that was as likely as pigs flying over a blue moon on the twelfth of never. Chasse was understandably anxious.

Dotty, the youngest of the Oglesby clan, lay on her back among the packages on the cottony green tree-skirt deep within the underbelly of the Christmas tree. Also on his back, Dawnet lay right beside her. Dawnet was a giant among Cairn Terriers towering nearly a full twelve inches at his withers, more brass than wheaten in coat and a tad more wiry. Both stared wondrously up at the juniper branches. Pencil in hand, open spiral notebook for a blanket, Dotty was deep in thought.

Dawnet's thoughts weren't even remotely deep. Since the fuzzy haired Terrier became part of the Oglesby pack, he had developed a special affinity for Dotty. It could have been because her hair and his fur were virtually the same color or because she played with him more than anybody else ever did or maybe just because they grew up together. Whatever his reasons, Dawnet had somehow decided it was his job to protect Dotty from all the dark forces loosed in the world like rolled newspapers and mailmen —or *that* cat.

That cat was a honey brown tabby named Marmalade who as far as Dawnet could tell didn't even understand Christmas. For instance, Marmalade did not appreciate the festive water bowl the family would bring out for the holiday. They would stick a tree in it but humans were always sticking things in their drinks. It did give the water an interesting flavor, he supposed, but he could take it or leave it.

Marmalade, of course, being a stupid cat did not understand it was a water bowl. She would actually climb into the tree garnish and knock off ornaments the humans had spent hours placing up there. When she did, it upset the whole pack. And no wonder. Decorations raining down from the tree garnish like that posed a serious hazard to the other pack members. That's what Dawnet thought they were doing now; watching for falling Christmas tree ornaments. There was also a suspicious looking gold ribbon on one of the packages that he had an eye on. Ribbons could be very sketchy.

Marmalade was nowhere close to Dawnet's festive water bowl and his tree garnish. She was warming herself by the fireplace. In her opinion, it was one of the few positives in a cascading list of negatives that surrounded this time of year. Always the same too. Nobody sat still long enough for her to warm herself on them. Strangers kept popping in day and night, disrupting her sleep. Her humans kept yelling at her for using that tree ladder the way it was meant to be used or whacking the ornaments, keepsakes, knickknacks and other toys now cluttering up the tree ladder as well as her whole territory.

None of this was her fault, mind you, and none of it would stop until the tree ladder was gone. Ah well, thought Marmalade, all the tempting sweets left lying around the house were sure to attract a mouse —if it ever quieted down, that is. Then at least she might catch herself a treat.

Dana, the oldest daughter and a true techno geek, was sprawled across the sofa with her laptop. She should have looked like a slob. Her hair was wadded carelessly and clipped to the top of her head. Her feet were stuffed in dirty pink dust mop slippers, her jeans had never seen an iron and her sweat shirt was big enough for three people. On anyone else, it would have been ugly. On her, it was shabby chic. Maybe because she was a natural beauty. Maybe because she just didn't care. The girl was closing a business deal.

Dana's laptop screen read: PU RN. PAY L8R. (Pickup Right Now. Pay Later.)

Dana typed: No. PU RN. Pay RN. (If you pickup right now, you pay right now.)

The reply: RN???? (Right now? Really?)

She typed: Yes.

The reply: W8 N Front H? (Wait for me in front of your house?)

Dana: No. Knock.

The reply: I C UR MA ??? (What if I see your mother?)

Dana typed: LI (Lie, you idiot.)

The reply: KK CUS (Okay; Okay. See you soon.)

Then the phone rang in loud crisp, golden trills.

Chasse's job description included answering the phone. In fact, any task that was thankless or demeaning was her job. Chasse stopped dinner setup and started for the phone hiding in the far corner of the great room. She hadn't even cleared the dining area when Debbie, the Oglesby middle child, bounded down the stairs and pounced on the ringing phone. She had it off the hook and answered before Chasse even blinked.

Debbie was about as opposite Dana as a sister could be and still be related. She was just as pretty, a little chubby, always meticulously dressed, her long hair carefully styled and her feelings right there on her sleeve for all the world to see. Disgust and disappointment registered on her face the very second she recognized Malynda Piper's voice. "He's not here," Debbie was ready to hangup.

"I'm your father's boss." Malynda assumed the child would be more respectful once she understood how important Malynda was. Not a chance.

"He's still not here," Debbie replied.

"Is your mother..?" Malynda began.

"She's not here either," Debbie was succinct to the edge of rude. Fortunately for her, Malynda didn't know the difference.

"Is there anybody there..?" Malynda tried again.

"Nobody." Debbie didn't want anybody tying up that phone. She had her reasons.

"Could you tell your father..?"

"I guess."

Debbie hung up the phone and raced upstairs.

"Who was that, Debbie?" Chasse chased her.

"Nobody!" She vanished to her lair beyond the top landing. Ordinarily, Debbie kept a secret the way a sieve holds water. But today she was too upset to talk.

Chasse stopped at the bottom landing and called after her, "Didn't sound like nobody."

"If Little Dee says it was nobody, it was nobody." Grampy defended all of his grandchildren even when they were right.

"Yeah," said Dana. "Disembodied people call here all the time."

"I just hope Mrs. Oglesby gets home soon," Chasse returned to the dining table. "Busses don't run late on Christmas Eve."

At Hamelin toys, Malynda was marching to the elevator. That call to the Oglesby house put her in a mood. Passing the copier, she noticed Zwang sprawled across the top of the machine. She marched back, leaned close to his ear and in a voice that would shred a whiteboard screamed, "Zwang!"

Zwang immediately tumbled off the copier to the floor and flopped around like a bearded catfish on a river bank. The little fat Santa was suddenly sober and scared out of his wits. He grappled with his pants tangled around his ankles in a futile struggle to cover his privates.

Malynda looked down on him and smiled. "Better update your resumé, Zwang." She continued to the elevator. Malynda glanced over at the janitor who quickly looked down. Werner had good reflexes. She kicked one of the filled trash bags out of her path and punched the elevator button. In an almost conscious act of self preservation, the elevator doors opened immediately. Malynda stepped in. She was on her way.

Chapter 6:

A Foggy Christmas Eve

As night fell so did everything else. Especially the temperature. Falling snow sparkled in the headlamps of Johnetta Hoyle's Jeep and the glowing windows of the gated community's guard shack. The distant snow covered rooftops of the micro-mansions in the streetlights beyond gave a Currier and Ives feel to the place. Johnetta's charge sat quietly shivering in the backseat wrapped in a gray wool coat with a seatbelt strapped around her. The car heater was going full blast but fingers of cold creeped in and chilled the young girl anyway. Still the girl said nothing. "She could use a better coat," Johnetta thought, then promptly forgot all about it.

The hazy picture window of the guard shack looked like a Monet painting in bad light. Johnetta couldn't make out anything but she watched anyway. The glass of the guard shack was as fogged as her windshield. Anything warm with glass wrapped around it was fogging over. Finally, the door opened and the guard came back wielding her list and his clipboard. She rolled her window halfway down, far enough to let winter flood in while they talked.

"Sorry, Ms. Hoyle," the guard's words puffed out in little clouds of vapor, "Looks like everybody is gone for the Holidays."

"The Weils?" Ms. Hoyle puffed back.

"Gone for the Holidays."

"The Heldoorns?"

"Gone for the Holidays."

"Even the Faistenowers?"

"Gone. Oh, wait a minute," The guard ran a gloved thumb down the list. "Faistenowers not on here. Let me check." The private guard returned to his shack. Johnetta Hoyle and her charge sat in the cold dark for another moment watching the very air fog. At last, the guard walked back out.

"The Faistenowers say they're gone for the Holidays too."

Johnetta ignored the absurdity. She smiled and thanked the guard. He returned to his shack. She rolled up the window and thumbed the redial on her BlackBerry. Her assistant answered. "Do we know anyone who doesn't live in a gated community?" she asked.

Chapter 7:

Perspectives

There is never a point to the underbelly of a Christmas tree. Dotty and Dawnet decided to take their problem to the smartest person in the world. "Grampy," Dotty asked, "is there really a Santa Claus?"

"Don't believe a thing he says, Dotty," Dana proclaimed from her couch kingdom.

"She's right, Kiddo," Grampy said. "You can't trust anybody on Christmas Eve."

"But you wouldn't lie, Grampy," Dotty mounted his chair arm while Dawnet rolled on his back beneath the recliner's pop-out footrest. The little dog preferred his world upside down.

"Everybody lies, little sister," Dana said. "Grampy is just honest about it."

"Shut up, Dana! You don't know!" Dotty was a child and children believe in things like adults until life teaches them differently.

"Oh, she knows, Kiddo," Grampy winked a nod. "You're at the age with all the questions. Dana is at the age with all the answers."

"What age are you at, Grampy?" asked Dotty.

"The age of Bonanza," Grampy sighed.

"So is there a Santa, Grampy?"

"It's a little late in the season to start doubting Santa, don't you think?" Grampy squelched a grin. "I mean we're already in the tank."

"It's the time thing, Grampy," Dotty said. "It doesn't make sense."

"Time thing?" Grampy stared quizzically at his little grand-daughter.

Ever the little scientist, Dotty opened her notebook, folded it back and used her pencil like a pointer. The ruled page was crowded with numbers, algebra equations, stick figures and even a freehand bar graph and histogram. A couple of doodles of

Dawnet graced the margins of the page as well. The little girl had done her homework.

"In the United States alone," she began," you have one hundred and fifty million families distributed over four million square miles. Even if you completely discounted the rest of the world and presumed an Eastern heading to take full advantage of the time change, of course…"

"Of course," agreed Grampy.

"…My figures show Santa would still have to cover one hundred and thirty eight miles per second to reach every household in one night. That is not even considering present delivery. Now, once you add in the rest of the world…"

"Hold it, Dotty," Dana actually looked up from her computer, "Let me get this straight. You have no trouble with flying reindeer, bottomless toy sacks, a guy who lives in the subzero arctic with elves. In fact, you have no trouble with elves at all or a fat man squeezing through a six inch stove pipe; But one guy being everywhere in the world in one night —that's the deal breaker for you? That's the part you can't believe?"

"Your point?" asked Dotty.

"I have to be adopted," laughed Dana.

"Don't mind Dana," Grampy said. "What do you think the answer could be?"

"A conspiracy, Grampy," Dotty's demeanor shifted to a quiet confidential, "the size and scope of which we can only begin to imagine."

"A conspiracy?" Grampy matched her tone. "Of who?"

"All the parents in the world," she concluded. "You think it's possible?"

"Well, Kiddo," Grampy answered, "All I ever get for Christmas is socks and cashews. Sure sounds like your ma. Then again, if it was your ma, it's a miracle I get cashews."

"If it is a conspiracy of parents," Dotty said, "our Christmas presents must be somewhere in this very house."

"You mean," Grampy looked truly astonished, "at this very moment?"

Dotty nodded solemnly. "Will you help me hunt for them, Grampy?"

"And settle the Santa question?" Grampy said with all the seriousness he could summon. "I'm with you all the way, Kiddo. You make a list of places to search. I got one little thing to take care of first and then I'm all yours."

Dotty flipped to a blank sheet in her notebook. A new list required a new page. Her assistant, Dawnet, joined her back in the underbelly of the Christmas tree.

The telephone rang again. More golden trills. Chasse was in the kitchen. This time, she ran. Didn't matter. Debbie leaped down the stairs and on the phone, waving her away. Debbie was so sure who it was but it wasn't. It was Johnetta Hoyle. Debbie was almost too crestfallen to speak.

"Your mother home?" Johnetta asked.

"Nope," Debbie said.

"Gone for the holidays?" Johnetta asked.

"Nope," Debbie said again.

"Good. Tell your mother I'm coming by," Johnetta talked just like the world wasn't coming to an end which Debbie knew it was.

"I guess," Debbie quietly hung up the handset. She stood there, staring at the phone until Chasse broke the spell.

"Who was that, Debbie?"

In tears, Debbie tore up the stairs to her room. Not even Grampy could stop her.

"It's that silly boy," Dana said. "He hasn't called her since she lost her cell."

"What happen to her cell?" asked Grampy.

"She ran over her minutes again," Chasse answered. " So Mrs. Oglesby said, 'I'm the Queen of Cell Phones,' and revoked her cell privileges."

"You were right there in your chair when Mom did it, Grampy," Dana said.

"Must of been during Bonanza," Grampy's number two excuse for missing or forgetting anything. Red Sox game was his number one.

"It's her own fault, anyway," Dana went on. "I showed her how to steal minutes, social engineer billing, even use Dad's card but she won't listen."

"Yawp," Grampy nodded. "It's hard to imagine how she could possibly get into a fix with you as her moral compass."

"I don't think she's all that mad about the phone anyway," Dana was already retreating to her laptop. "She knew Mom was going to take it."

"But to do it so close to Christmas," Chasse said. "There's already too much drama."

"Yeah, well, she'll be all better when her little Grubworm comes by." That's what Dana called Arnold Ogden Grubb Junior, the boy in question. Then again, that's what everybody called Arnold Ogden Grubb Junior, except for Debbie.

"I just hope nothing on those calls makes me late," Chasse checked her watch. "I got to catch that bus."

Chasse headed back into the kitchen to a fully loaded stove. She removed the turkey from the main oven, checked the bread in the warmer and started moving food to the serving dishes.

Dotty and Dawnet popped into the kitchen. The dog took a moment to sniff the floor for any food droppings. You could never tell when something delicious might have fallen on the floor so it was always pertinent to check.

"Chasse," asked Dotty, notebook and pencil at the ready, "in your travels around the house, did you ever see anything wrapped in fancy paper and bows with maybe a candy cane taped to it?"

"Not with my name on it!" Chasse could deadpan with the best of them.

Two mellow bongs. Of course the doorbell rang, Chasse thought. She spun out of the kitchen, Dotty and Dawnet at her heels. Debbie was already flying down the stairs and through the great room to the foyer. Chasse just made the foyer in time to see Debbie fling the front door wide open. Snow and a snow dusted parka wrapped around a large plastic tray rushed in. Debbie slammed the door after. She could smell who it was.

"Merry Christmas, Mrs. Baklava!" Debbie shouted.

Mrs. Baklava was actually Beck Lovat, their next door neighbor. She had been after Grampy for about as long as the two youngest girls could remember. She made absolutely the best tasting baklava on the entire planet. Best smelling too. In all the time Beck knew the Oglesbys, nobody in the family ever called her by her name. Except Grampy—when she could catch him.

While Beck was Merry Christmas-ing her way from the foyer into the great room, Grampy was dropping the remote, sliding out of his chair and slipping through the breakfast nook down the back hall to his room. Dotty quickly took his place in the recliner. Dawnet hopped up after her. Marmalade, the only true Ninja in the household, had vanished the moment Debbie put her hand on the door handle. Marmalade knew there was nothing on the other side of that door she was the least bit interested in and dealt with it accordingly. She hid.

"Where's your Grandfather?" Beck asked.

"Where he always is," Debbie, pointed to the back of his easy chair. Before Beck could even start toward Grampy's chair, Debbie shot back upstairs.

At the recliner, Beck was not all that surprised to see only a smiling Dotty all leaned back holding the channel changer, a tail wagging Dawnet stretched out beside her. "Merry Christmas, Mrs. Baklava."

"Merry Christmas, Little Dot," Beck's eyes swiveled around. "Where's your Grandfather?"

"He had to go, Mrs. Baklava," Dotty gushed.

"Oh?" Beck may have flinched a little.

"He's an old guy. They have to go a lot."

"Oh," Beck missed him again. "I brought over these baklava and.."

"Oh, the pastries!" Chasse ran over and took the tray. "Thank you so much."

"You're welcome, so much," Beck was pleased someone was glad to see her.

"Are you staying for supper, Mrs. Baklava?" Chasse carried the tray to the breakfast nook.

"No Chasse," Beck answered. "I was hoping to catch Mr. Oglesby."

"Dragging Grampy Coy to the New Year's ball, huh?" Chasse finished setting up the tray.

"I wouldn't call it 'dragging', but today is the last day for tickets." Every New Year, the Community Center had a dance and, every New Year, Beck had to cajole Grampy into going. Maybe it wasn't dragging but there was a certain amount of force involved.

"Oh no," exclaimed Dotty. "Today's over, Mrs. Baklava."

"I get a few complimentary tickets, little Dot," Beck said. "I'm on the planning committee. Just wanted to make sure your Grandfather was coming."

"You do this every year with him, Mrs. Baklava." Chasse headed back to the kitchen. "Why not find some man who likes to dance."

"At my age," laughed Beck, "It's hard enough to find some man."

"Don't pay any attention to Chasse," Dana said. "You are about the only exercise Grampy gets."

"Dancing is good exercise," Beck observed.

"No, I mean the running and the hiding."

Chapter 8:

All That and a Can of Popcorn

Everyone in the house stopped. Even Dawnet. There was a loud rolling rumble like a roller coaster in free fall punctuated by the rusty creak of neglected hinges and ending in a shuddering thump. The garage door had opened. No one moved. A moment of silence then the whole racket began again. Debbie appeared on the landing. Rolling rumble, plaintive rusty creak, shuddering thump. The garage door was closed. At the second shuddering thump, the girls all shouted in unison: "Mommy's home!" The children and terrier ran to the breakfast nook as their mom entered from the garage.

Briefcase and purse in hand, Darla hadn't even cleared the entrance when her two youngest grabbed her. Dotty hugged her below the waist.

Debbie hugged her above. Dawnet orbited them, barking joyfully. Darla made it to the credenza with both girls in tow and Dawnet weaving through her legs. She set down her purse and briefcase. Dana was much too mature to go chasing after mom anymore. She did stand and smile a moment. Then, remembering herself, hurriedly dropped back on the sofa to be unenthusiastically disinterested. Regardless, she was just as happy as her sisters mom was home.

Darla managed to pry her parka off and continue shuffling forward with both girls clamped to her and a doggy satellite orbiting.

Beck Lovat watched in utter amazement. "It's so obvious you're a parent."

"Oh, your pastries!" Darla exclaimed in genuine delight. "That's so nice, Mrs. Baklava. Merry Christmas!"

"Mrs. Oglesby," said Chasse, "please remember I have to go early tonight. Buses don't run late on Christmas…"

"Chasse," Darla cut her off, "I have groceries in the car."

Chasse frowned and started for the garage.

"Staying for dinner, Mrs. Baklava?" Darla asked.

"She's not staying, Mrs. Oglesby," Chasse called back as she left.

"I just came over to see Coy," Beck said.

"He should be in his chair," Darla hobbled to the great room. "I swear, he does nothing but sit in front of that TV all day."

"I can see you're a little busy." Beck headed for the foyer. "I can come back."

"You really should stay for dinner," Darla followed Beck, no small task wrapped in clinging girls and their little dog too.

Debbie remembered one of the calls. "Mommy, Ms. Hoyle is coming over."

"Chasse didn't take the call?" Darla asked.

"Chasse wasn't fast enough," Dotty said.

It was at that moment, Beck Lovat opened the front door. Out of a blizzard of snow, Johnetta Hoyle swooped in like an abominable Sasquatch, a large round Christmas tin of popcorn in her arms.

Beck pushed the door closed. Johnetta stomped off the excess snow collected on her feet and shoulders, leaving it to melt in pools on the foyer floor as she strutted into the Oglesby's home like she owned the place. Understandable since Johnetta Hoyle owned most of the places she strutted into.

Dawnet aimed a couple of well placed barks directly at Johnetta, just in case no one else noticed they were being invaded by something the size of a small polar bear.

"My, oh me!" Johnetta shivered. "Too cold out for man or beast."

"Apparently, not all beasts." Dana's little asides were generally ignored by everyone but her mother and sisters which is precisely why she did them.

Usually Though, Johnetta Hoyle could be easily offended by almost anything and anyone. However in this particular instance, she was more concerned with Beck Lovat. "What are you doing here, Beck?" Her voice had enough growl, it even scared the dog.

"I live next door," Beck was unfazed. "What are you doing here, Johnny?"

"Bringing comfort and joy to all God's creatures," Johnetta preachified with more than a little affectation.

"On Christmas Eve?" Dana couldn't help herself. "Isn't there a no stirring rule among the creatures?"

"Johnetta," Darla jumped in, "you have to stay for supper." She called out to Chasse staggering in from the garage under a mountain of grocery bags. "Chasse! Set another place for Ms. Hoyle!"

"If she's staying, I'm staying!" Beck studied Johnetta for a reaction.

"Chasse!" Darla called again, "Set two places!"

Chasse dumped the groceries in the kitchen floor and raided the cupboards for two more place settings. She knew no amount of eye rolling was going to save her.

"Nice of you to offer, Darla," Johnetta eyeballed Beck back, "but it is Christmas Eve. We've all have places to be."

Chasse was nodding in agreement as she plunked down two more settings at the dining table.

"Well, if she's not staying, I'm not staying," Beck was fine with toe to toe.

"Chasse!" called Darla.

"I heard, Mrs. Oglesby," Chasse left both place settings anyway. Chasse had been back and forth in this family long enough to know there is no back. She returned to the kitchen. There were all those groceries to put away.

Johnetta fished the gold business card case from her purse. "First things first," she announced, passing out business cards. "I posted a reward for any information leading to the capture and arrest of the Pod Pirate."

"Mobius Dick!" Darla, Beck Lovat and the two youngest girls all shouted with glee. They immediately started laughing. The fact they said it at the exact same time tickled them. The fact they said it at all annoyed Johnetta. She swallowed her contempt and continued passing out business cards.

"The Pod Pirate," Johnetta emphasized the name, "is real. If any of you see or hear anything, anything at all, and at any time, please call me. I posted a reward." Beck Lovat smirked at Johnetta's fancy business card the moment she got it. Johnetta noticed and snatched it back. "Shouldn't you be next door now, Beck?"

"It's Mrs. Baklava," said Debbie.

"She's here to see Grampy," added Dotty.

"So Ms. Hoyle, you looking for a little Grampy action too? asked Dana.

"No," Johnetta was terse. "Never. Not after last year's Ball."

"Grampy Coy wasn't untoward was he?" Darla always feared the worst with that old man.

"A decent woman can't say," Johnetta barely concealed her contempt.

"I can," Beck was busting happy to. "Coy compared her to the ball."

"Compared her to the New Year's dance?"

"No," said Beck. "The actual physical ball they drop at midnight."

At the previous New Year's ball, Johnetta Hoyle showed up at the Community Center in a grandiose roaring twenties styled mirror sequined satin tube dress with matching skull cap, coin purse and sling back heels. It would have looked great on any girl a third Johnetta's age and size. But a very rotund older woman standing there in the middle of the dance floor beneath a matching mirrored ball was unfortunate if not out and out bad luck.

"That's terrible, Johnetta," What else could Darla say to the most influential person in town?

"And she was with him!" snapped Johnetta, pointing a chubby finger at Beck.

"I just dance with the man," Beck chided. "I don't control his mouth."

"You were laughing," scolded Johnetta. "She was laughing," Johnetta turned to Darla, a touch too tearful to be believed.

"Mrs. Baklava!" Darla feinted a shocked response because, again, the most important person in town was playing the victim.

"Served Her right," Beck gave up on any civility and went straight for her old friend's jugular. "She wouldn't leave Coy alone all night. And that dress was not a good look for most people. Sure wasn't a good look for you, Johnny."

"Like you're some fashionista," Johnetta didn't lie down for anybody. "It was supposed to be trendy. Fun. À La Mode."

"I scream. You scream. We all scream..," Dana amused only herself. Maybe her sisters.

"You ought to be able to express yourself any way you want, Johnetta; freedom of expression." Darla believed one should never speak ill of a faux pas when walking on eggshells.

"You know it's freedom of expression when it is both free and dumb." Dana felt most rag rats were either peacocks, peasants or parrots in need of help. Making fun of them was her kind of intervention. No thanks required. She was glad to do it.

"Let me apologize for Grampy." Darla decided sacrificing her father-in-law might appease them and the fashion gods. "That old man only does two things: Sit in front of that TV all day and insult people."

"He was just having fun, Darla. And it was nigh on a year ago. You would think you would be over it, Johnny." Beck wasn't one to lie down either.

"I'm a sensitive person, Beck. At least mindful of others," Johnetta Hoyle treaded dangerously close to sermonizing. "You know how I'm always thinking of others, Darla. All I ask in return is a little consideration."

"I know I'm giving her little consideration." Dana truly was.

Throwing Grampy under the bus clearly did not work. Darla needed to change the subject before victimhood became haranguing and haranguing fomented into a little war. Beck would stop if Johnetta stopped. "What brought you all the way out here in a snowstorm anyway, Johnetta?"

"Our Home for the Holidays program," Johnetta changed instantly from little Miss Muffet to spider.

"Oh no, Johnetta." And Darla changed instantly from tuffet to fly. "I never volunteered."

"I specifically remember you said we could call on you anytime."

"For a donation, Johnetta."

"That's all I'm asking, Darla. A donation of your time." Johnetta was an expert in the art of coercion.

She practiced every day. No little fly stood a chance.

"It's Christmas Eve," Darla hoped playing the Christmas card would work.

"Any time is any time, Mom," Dana was not helping.

"Now, you're on her side?" Darla knew the answer. Dana wasn't on anybody's side. She was just having fun.

"I have this one little homeless girl, sweet as pie," Johnetta was making the pitch.

"Johnetta, you can't come to someone at the last possible minute…" Darla began a counter pitch.

"She has no place to go, Darla," Johnetta wasn't buying. She was selling. "And it would be so nice for her to see how a normal family celebrates Christmas."

"Can I come?" asked Dotty.

Debbie pulled Dotty aside, "By normal, she means us."

Dotty mouthed an "Oh" even as the consigning of the popcorn tin began.

First Johnetta passed the tin to Darla. "You don't even have to buy her a present," meaning the big popcorn tin would suffice.

"That's good since it's absolutely too late to get one," Darla shoved the popcorn tin back at Johnetta, meaning: No.

"I'm not asking you to do anything hard," Johnetta pushed the popcorn tin back to Darla. "Just open your heart and home on Christmas."

"To a complete stranger?" Darla pushed the popcorn tin back to Johnetta. "I don't know anything about this girl."

"She's a little quirky," Johnetta pushed the popcorn tin at Darla and sped away, "but completely harmless. She stayed with the Novaks last year and the Heldoorns for a couple of Christmases before that." Johnetta kept arm's length away from Darla and the popcorn tin.

"So why isn't she spending this Christmas with one of them?" Darla and the popcorn tin pursued Johnetta around the sofa. It was amazing a woman that huge could be so nimble in stiletto heels.

"Oddly, they're both gone for the Holidays this year," Now Johnetta ducked behind Beck.

"So why don't you..?" Darla paused from the chase. Johnetta was just too agile.

"Oh, I'm gone for the Holidays too. Or I would. Any decent person would." Johnetta was dressing down Darla with her eyes. "My oh me, Darla. I'm just asking you to open your heart to one poor little girl on Christmas Eve. You'd think you would have a touch of compassion on the Holidays."

Darla gave the popcorn tin to Debbie who happily skipped it over to their Christmas tree and plunked it down among the other gifts. Darla hadn't been shamed into anything. Just giving up. There's that moment the rabbit knows it's caught.

"So where is this little girl now?" asked Darla.

"Outside," said Johnetta.

"Outside!" cried Beck, Darla and the girls as they ran for the foyer. So much for Ms. Hoyle's sensitivity and consideration.

Darla flung open the door.

In a shimmering blitz of snow powder, a long, lanky, bone thin teenager in crocheted cap, mittens, oversized blanket coat, mismatched boon dockers and a faded green polyester dress stood quietly shivering to death on their doorstep, large carpet bag over one shoulder and a child's tiny cracked vinyl clutch purse in her hand. Beck and Darla each took an arm and pulled her inside as Debbie closed the door behind them.

Beck brushed the snow from the girl as Darla handed the clutch purse to Dotty. Debbie took her bag. Darla removed the girl's mittens and started rubbing and blowing on her hands to warm them as they quickly led the girl over to the fireplace.

"Are you alright?" Darla asked the girl. She might have nodded. No one could be sure because she was shaking so violently.

"This is not a little girl, Johnny!" Beck asserted.

"Her name is Candice Siwel," Johnetta announced like it explained everything.

"C-c-c-call m-me C-C-Candy," the girl gasped.

"Nice to meet you, Candy." Darla worked on the girl's icy fingers. "Let's warm you up."

Suddenly from the girl came a high pitched very short mouselike squeak. After all those early years of practice, it was second nature for her now. Any emotions requiring some sort of physical release like laughter, crying or surprise, that was all she would do. Squeak.

"I am absotively related to be here," Candy spoke barely above a whisper.

"What?" Dotty wasn't sure she heard right.

"Candice has a rather unique vocabulary," Johnetta soft-pedaled. "You'll get used to it."

"Squeak!" laughed Candy or at least for her what passed as laughing. "You guys are gonna use my vocapillary?"

"Is a vocapillary the one that flows to the heart or from the heart?" asked Dotty. "I always get them confused."

"I think it's the one that joins the others together," Debbie reckoned.

"Not in this case, dear," Darla noticed Johnetta backing away.

"That must be why it's unique," Dotty reasoned.

"I have to be adopted." Dana was certain her gene pool came from an entirely different ocean than her sisters. Shuffling chromosomes alone couldn't begin to explain the disparity.

"See? You all understand each other already," Johnetta bolted for the door. Darla chased her only to the threshold. She watched from the Foyer as Johnetta Hoyle bustled down to her big Jeep Cherokee like a polar bear to an ice floe, bellowing all the way. "This will be that poor child's last Christmas before she ages out of the system so please make it a nice one." Johnetta called from the SUV, "We'll be by for her after New Year's!"

"After New Year's!?!" Darla wasn't ready to have a guest for one night, let alone over a week.

"Merry Christmas!" Johnetta shouted as she rolled a window down and up and pumped her engine to a roar. The jeep sped off, crunching all the way. The tires didn't even slip. That woman couldn't be human.

Darla closed the door, stilled herself then stepped back into the great room.

"Dana," she ordered. "Show our guest to her room so she can get settled before supper."

"Mom, I'm on my laptop," Dana's justification for not doing anything. It never worked. That didn't stop her from using it.

"And I am the queen of laptops," Darla said.

"I'm going. I'm going," None of the kids argued with their mother when she declared she was queen of something. To do so would always end badly. Instead, Dana put her laptop on the coffee table, yanked Candy's bag from Debbie then led a forced march up the stairs. Her sisters each took one of Candy's hands and followed.

"Hope you like it here," called Darla as the girls mounted the stairs.

"B-b-better than out there," replied Candy in a voice quiet as a shiver.

"You think that now," Dana announced as their little troop reached the landing.

"Why do you put up with her?" asked Beck.

"She's my daughter," Darla's gaze followed the girls until they disappeared off the landing.

"Not Dana," Beck replied more than a little amused. "Johnny Hoyle."

"Johnetta Hoyle is the biggest woman in town," Darla couldn't believe the question.

"Granted but size isn't everything," Beck joked.

"I mean, Mrs. Baklava, Johnetta heads the Board of supervisors, PTA and every local chapter of any private everything in the County."

"She's certainly the big ordure at CACA-POO."

"Well, I need my CPA license and Johnetta controls all that."

"I thought you worked as a CPA," Beck could see the exasperation in Darla's face.

"I do," said Darla, "but the only way up is out. Working for a company, you just need a degree. Working for yourself, you need a license."

Like most everyone else in town who worked for a living, Darla couldn't afford to be on Johnetta's bad side. Beck was immune only because she was retired and Johnetta Hoyle's best friend. She also knew the rich socialite better than anybody. Beck gave Darla's arm a light squeeze. "You don't have to worry about Johnny," Beck promised. "She can be intimidating and pretentious as hell, but she's always fair."

It was at that moment Chasse walked in with a plain white bag. "Mrs. Oglesby, I don't know where to put this."

"I know where I'd like to put it." Darla took the bag and turned back to her neighbor. "Speaking of which, want me to find Coy for you, Mrs. Baklava?"

"That's alright," Beck headed for the foyer. "I'll check on Coy later." Darla watched Mrs. Baklava depart through the front door into a fog of snow.

"Mrs Oglesby, my bus…" Chasse started to plead with all the desperation of someone who didn't want to walk home alone in the dark during a snow storm.

Darla interrupted with all the desperation of someone who didn't want to deal with anything extra she didn't have to. "Chasse, please take some blankets and towels up to our guest."

Chasse was disappearing up the stairs when Grampy was reappearing from the downstairs hallway by the breakfast nook. Darla fetched the plain white bag over to him. "I hope you didn't make me buy my own Christmas gift."

"Nawp." Grampy checked the contents and squished out a grin. "Wouldn't waste your money." He and the bag vanished back down the corridor to his bedroom.

A sudden loud rolling rumble drowned by screeching metal filled the house. Darla waited quietly. There was the shuddering thump. Then silence. Hardly a minute later, another rumble and plaintive squeal of a dying garage door sliding closed rippled through the house and stopped just as suddenly in a final stuttering thump. Darla smiled and hurried to the breakfast nook. She was there when Dan came in from the garage. Just seeing her made him smile.

"Darn it, Darla! Nothing like a nice, quiet Christmas Eve at home," he said.

Darla hugged and kissed him. "So far, this certainly has been nothing like it."

Chapter 9:

From Your Lips to God's Ear

Dotty's bedroom was an enchanted world where sciences and arts shared equal floor space with the denizens of make believe. A framed classic 1939 Wizard of Oz movie poster adorned with little red slippers hung on one sky blue wall while an Einstein poster and the periodic table were thumb tacked to another. A twin bed occupied the window wall with an assortment of shoes and dog toys tossed carelessly beneath. Stuffed into the corner at the foot of the bed was an absolutely pristine high quality doggy bed that had never ever been even touched by a dog. Not ever. A toy box wedged against a full dresser was stuffed with dirty clothes while the dresser top itself like the rest of the room played host to dolls, books, puzzles, games and unfinished projects. Disorder was sprinkled liberally on everything.

Dana walked into Dotty's realm, tossed Candy's bag into one of the corners, toe brushed a path through the child clutter to Dotty's bed and collapsed on the dog hair covered comforter. Dotty and Dawnet were right behind with Debbie and Candy after.

"Hey, watch where you're throwing stuff," Dotty shouted, picking up Candy's bag and gingerly placing it atop the pile of things on her dresser. It was impossible to put the carpet bag anywhere in that room without setting it on a pile of things. The least cluttered place in the whole room was Dotty's bed and Dana was now occupying that.

"You can sleep here, Candy," Dana slapped the bed almost affectionately like a trusty steed.

"Hey, where am I going to sleep?" shouted Dotty who just as a normal course of action screamed at her oldest sister.

"With your sister," replied Dana.

"You're both my sisters," quipped Dotty.

"Ah, but only Debbie will admit it," Dana wangled a finger.

"Shuckydern!" shouted Debbie who likewise as a normal course of action screamed at the oldest as well, "Why can't she double up with you?"

"You're smaller," Dana said. "More room in your bed."

"Guys. Guys," Candy spoke so softly they had to stop shouting and actually listen, "I don't want to be an inquisition." She cleared a spot on the floor. "I can sleep here."

"I guess," Debbie nodded at Dotty.

"She can't sleep on the floor," Dana replied.

"It's okay," Candy said. "I sleep on floors a lot.

"Nobody's sleeping on the floor, Candy," Dana was firm.

"Why not, if she wants to?" Debbie was more arguing than asking.

"Yes, Dana, why not?" Dotty was more whining than arguing but arguing nonetheless.

"Ask mom," Dana knew full well that, at least for her kid sisters, their mother was the court of final appeal and that court wouldn't make anyone sleep on the floor on a cold winter's night.

"Ooooh," Dotty and Debbie both knew the discussion was over.

"So you are sleeping in a bed tonight, Candy," Dana continued. "You two make some space for her clothes."

The girls cleared a drawer in Dotty's dresser.

"Tenably a-grease-able," Candy whispered, "but I could sleep on the floor. It's a perfectly exceptionable a-manatee. Mommy and me used to do it all the time."

"Where's your mommy?" asked Dotty.

"She had to go to Heaven," Candy was cheerful as ever.

"Sorry Candy," Dana sat up. "We didn't know."

"Oh, it's alright," Candy's voice was forever soft. "I don't mind. I was real little when Mommy had to go to Heaven. And she told me: If you got to go somewhere, Candy, Heaven is the best place in the world to go."

Suddenly, there was a distant rumble of old roller bearings buried in the screech of old rust. The girls and Dawnet stopped. In total bewilderment, Candy looked around at them as a loud thump shook the bedroom. No one moved. Shortly, the rumble and squeaking metal started again and ended with another huge thump.

"Daddy's home!" The three girls shouted in unison and Dawnet barked once then the spell was broken and they continued on as if nothing had happened.

Dotty and Debbie had cleared a drawer and Candy began laying out her things to put away. A change of underwear. Then a toothbrush, a hair brush, a clothes brush, a shoe brush, a wire brush, a toilet brush, another hair brush and a Dandy brush —individually, one at a time. Brush after brush.

"Where do you stay?" asked Debbie.

"Wherever I can," whispered Candy.

"Why do you have so many brushes?" Dotty asked.

Candy answered as she put each brush carefully and lovingly in the drawer. "When I was little, Mommy would be brushing the tanglements out of my hair. I would cry sometimes because it hurt a little and she would say: Candy, brushes are our friends. And you can never have too many friends."

"They do look friendly," Dotty observed.

"Christmas must be really sad for you," Debbie imagined how hard and tragic Candy's life must be.

Candy's face exploded in a big smile and that little mouse squeak laughed out. "Squeak! My Christmas is always the merriest Christmas ever. Is your Christmas sad?

"No," said Debbie, "but I'm not homeless."

"Neither am I," Candy declared as loud as wind. "I'm home as much as I can be. If there's a home available, I'm in it. So I'm home more; never less."

"But is it your home or somebody else's?" Debbie was still imagining.

"Mine," said Candy, "until they make me leave. Ms. Hoyle says I'm dishin' french fries, but that ain't true. I never served french fries in my whole life."

"I've eaten them," Dotty volunteered, "Never served them though."

"She probably said 'disenfranchised', Candy," Dana posited. "You lose some rights if you don't have a legal residence."

"I had a lethal residence once, but I'm all cleared up now," Candy replied.

"Do you have a place to stay?" asked Debbie.

"Sure," Candy said. "Tonight, I'm staying here."

"You must not get very many presents," Dotty was getting to the crux of the matter.

There was that happy little squeak again. "Squeak! Do you get a big can of popcorn every year? Ms. Hoyle gets me a big can of popcorn every year."

"That's all she gets you? Popcorn?" Debbie pouted. At last, a hardship to be outraged over!

"Not just popcorn. Stale Popcorn," Candy sounded authentically delighted at the thought.

"You can't get popcorn that stale overnight. It takes a lot of aging, but Ms. Hoyle always comes through. Must take a lot of thought and planning."

"Doesn't sound like a wonderful gift," But Dotty wasn't a hundred percent certain. She had long ago worked out that a gift's wonderfulness was inversely proportional to its usefulness and exponentially related to the number of pieces involved. This made popcorn particularly difficult to figure out.

"Used to, I never got popcorn. Getting popcorn is pretty wonderful." Candy didn't require any formula to know something is better than nothing.

"So you stay with a different family every Christmas?" asked Debbie.

"Not every Christmas," Candy said. "But every Christmas, I'm always somewhere."

"Not every Christmas could be wonderful then," Dotty couldn't reconcile transience with Christmas gifts. Even if there was a Santa, he couldn't hope to locate her. "You must have some bad ones."

"We get everything we ask for," Debbie noted, "and we still have some pretty lame Christmases."

In truth, Debbie could count the number of perfectly un-lame Christmases in her life on one finger.

"Squeak!" came Candy's quick and joyous mouse laugh, "I have the merriest Christmas ever!"

"How?" asked Dotty. "If you don't even know where you are going to be on Christmas?"

Candy's whisper rose to an excited hush. "I have my own little Christmas magic. Looky!" From her little clutch purse, Candy pulled a cheap plastic silver bell ornament and presented it proudly as one would show off an invaluable keepsake or family heirloom.

"Aw, that's just an ornament," said Dotty.

"My mommy gave it to me the day she went to Heaven. Listen!" Candy's face filled with unsuppressed joy as she shook the little bell. The young girls listened intently.

Debbie strained. "I don't hear anything."

"Not a ding or a ring. Nothing," Dotty nodded.

"I know," whispered Candy, then, "Squeak! It doesn't have a tongue!"

"Tongue?" Dotty touched the tip of her own.

"Clapper," Dana told her kid sister. "It doesn't have a clapper like a real bell. It's an ornament."

"Bells without tongues can't talk," Candy shared her great secreted truth. "They can only listen. And Christmas Bells only listen for God."

Dana threw Candy a dubious look. "I think we are finally getting to the reason she's homeless."

Candy was not perturbed in the least. "Squeak! I know it sounds crazy but my mommy told me and she would never lie. On Christmas Eve, whatever you whisper into the little silver bell goes straight from your lips to God's ear."

"I'm so glad she's not sleeping in my room," Dana nudged her youngest sister.

"Straight from your lips to God's ear." Debbie had to ask, "What good is that?"

"God is everybody's daddy," Candy explained.

"Ah, so he's never around," Dana was being more hyperbolic than speaking from experience.

"Oh, no," But Candy was serious. "He's always around and he wants you to be happy, specially on Christmas."

"Is this like praying?" Dotty asked.

"I don't know." Candy replied. "I ask for something Christmas Eve. God sends it Christmas morning and ..Squeak! I have the merriest Christmas ever."

"What do you ask for?" Debbie was curious about what a person who has nothing would want.

"I don't know." Candy never really gave it much thought. "Different things." Candy's eyes pressed against the rim of her lids for a moment while she tried to remember something. "Oh," she said as a recollection floated into her brain. "You know how it preciprocates snow every year by Christmas. Well, one year, it hadn't preciprocated. Mister Rolle said it wasn't going to snow either. So I took out my little silver bell, cupped my hand around its rim and said 'Please God, make it snow.' And Squeak! Christmas morning, it snowed and I had the merriest Christmas ever."

"I don't believe it," Dana scoffed.

"I think it is true!" Debbie shouted.

"So do I!" Dotty was equally loud.

"Oh, the story is true. But it is not a miracle."

Both sisters yelled: "Shut up, Dana! You don't know!"

But Dana knew. At least, she thought she did. "Candy said herself, it always snows by Christmas. It would be more of a miracle, if it didn't snow."

"I bet Candy has another example." Dotty was all for empirical proof if it verified her suppositions.

"Sure," said Candy, "as soon as I can make one up."

"Shuckydern!" Debbie chimed in. "You don't need to. We believe you."

"We should test it then." Dana snatched the little Silver Bell ornament from Candy's fingers.

"Like a Make-my-true-love-come-for-me kind of test?" asked Debbie who never strayed far from worrying about her boy friend, Arnold Ogden Grubb Jr.

"Like a Doesn't-involve-your-smelly-little-boyfriend-in-any-way kind of test," Dana was not a fan of the Grubworm.

Now Candy's little squeak denoted trepidation. "Squeak! You can't test God. Mommy told me he doesn't like tests, not multiple choice, not even true or false."

Dotty reassured her. "It's okay Candy. We'll be good."

"Yeah, Candy," agreed Dana. "We'll be sincere."

"Arnold is not smelly," Debbie always defended Arnold's honor —though it had never been established that he had any.

"Oh yes," said Dotty. "He is." Grubworm's bouquet was an acquired taste like limburger in a mustard roll. Somebody might like it. Not Dotty. Not Dana. Not most people.

Dana cupped her hand around the Bell rim and made the first request: "Hey God. Make Dad appreciate the genius that I am." She smirked as she passed the bell to Dotty and said to no one in particular, "Yeah, that's gonna happen."

Dotty held the bell close to her lips and spoke with all the solemnity of an army radioman. "Dorothy to God. Dorothy to God. Come in, God."

"Don't ask for Dolls or anything silly," warned Debbie.

"Like Grubworm?" Dotty yelled back and then respectfully to the bell, "God, please make Daddy spend more time at home." She paused a second. "Over and Out!" She passed the bell to her sister.

Debbie took the bell, held it cupped in one hand. "Hello, God," she began. "Please fix it so Mom and Dad do more stuff together." She thought a second. "Even better, fix it so all of us do more stuff together."

"Now that is impossible," laughed Dana. "You can't name one thing we can all do as a family."

"Lunch!" Debbie handed the bell back to Candy.

A light knock and the bedroom door opened as Chasse took a step in the room with a stack of bed linens and a couple of towels. She threw the bed linens at Dana. "Mrs. Oglesby thought you should put these on the bed for Candy." She handed the towels to Candy. "Fresh towels so you can clean up, dear." Before Candy could respond, Chasse was off on her forced march to quitting time.

Dawnet jumped to his feet, even as the realization struck Dotty. "The linen closet!" she blurted to her four legged helper as she scooped up her notepad. Dawnet and Dotty scrambled out the bedroom door.

Debbie and Candy watched the door slam in total bewilderment. Completely un-flummoxed by it all, Dana hopped to her feet, tossed the sheets to her remaining sister and waved them both to the twin bed. "Come on Girls! This bed won't make itself."

Chapter 10:

Game Theory

"Cozy" is a realtor's term for "claustrophobically tiny". "Vintage" means "in desperate need of repair". And "Freestanding" is another way to say "not supported by anything at all". The Oglesby linen closet was a cozy room walled with vintage storage cabinets surrounding a muddle of freestanding shelves. Every iota of storage was crammed with towels, wash cloths, bed linen, table linens and even doilies. A few oddities like drop cloths, air filters and furniture covers were tucked into the narrow passages between open shelves around a vacuum cleaner, carpet cleaner and step ladder forming a little labyrinth of a maze. The place could have had it's own minotaur.

Dotty with her notebook and trusty assistant Dawnet stood in the opened doorway. She added 'linen closet' to the bottom of her list. Methodically working her way around the room, Dotty opened the first cabinet, rifled through the sheets on each shelf, closed the door after and opened the next cabinet to rifle through those things. And on she went searching for the presents she knew had to be somewhere.

It was clear to the keen deductive abilities of Dawnet as to what was going on. Dotty, he reasoned, was undoubtedly hunting. Perhaps a mouse or squirrel? Squirrel! That had to be it. First the tree garnish, then the bedroom and now the linen closet. What else could it be? Sadly, he did not smell one. In fact, he smelled nothing but cloth and appliances. Still Dawnet was a good pack member. If this was the game Dotty wanted to play, he would play too. Dawnet burrowed through the stacks of folded linens and boxes of cleaning supplies in the lower shelves of the floor units while Dotty searched all the cabinets and the upper shelves. Dawnet was determined to leave no bed sheet unturned in their great hunt for the Christmas squirrel.

Once the intrepid Cairn Terrier figured out the game, there was no stopping him. There was also no presents and no squirrels.

When they finished, the inside of every cabinet was disheveled, the shelf stacks now shelf piles and the floor an indiscriminate aggregation of things that should not ever be aggregated. Dotty looked over the mayhem they had wrought with a certain self-satisfaction and checked off 'linen closet' in her notebook. A good closet is always worth coming out of.

Together, little girl and little dog moved on. While Dana and Debbie helped their new guest get settled, Dotty and Dawnet completed their search of the entire upstairs bedrooms and closets. To Dotty's dismay, there were absolutely no Christmas presents anywhere to be found. Dawnet, on the other hand, had a wonderful time crawling under beds and burrowing through the bottoms of closets. It wasn't in vain either. He found a couple of snacks.

Chapter 11:

Always Bring The Whip

While Dotty and Dawnet were ravaging all the potential hiding places for Christmas squirrels, Grampy had done a fairly terrible job wrapping a gift. It was your typical small very square hatbox of assorted chocolates. It should have been easy to wrap but not one creased edge of the thick flocked paper was sharp, straight or flat making for a rumpled, misshapen package with long strips of cellophane tape stuck everywhere in no particular pattern, topped with a beautiful bow and gold gilded card. He set it in front of the Christmas tree like a magnificent work of art then returned to his chair and channel changer where he began his search for the only thing he ever watched outside of baseball —Bonanza.

Darla plonked down the stairs shouting for Chasse. They had just passed each other not ten minutes earlier. Chasse was running downstairs to finish her kitchen duties while Darla was running upstairs to check on the girls. What Darla found was catastrophe in the form of a tossed linen closet so naturally she started screaming. Chasse raced from the kitchen and caught her at the bottom landing.

"What is it, Mrs. Oglesby?" Chasse panted.

"The linen closet is completely trashed!" Darla was not what one would call composed.

"I was just there," Chasse's mouth hung open somewhere between dismay and astonishment.

"I know," Darla said in a tone very close to accusing.

"It was fine when I left," Chasse said in a tone very close to defensive.

"Well, it is not fine now." Darla replied in a tone very close to —no, it was exactly— accusatorial. "Fix it, Chasse." She offered no room for recourse. "I can't live with that through Christmas."

Chasse was flustered. Arguing would be a waste of time and time was something Chasse didn't have. She immediately marched upstairs.

Feeling a little more in control, Darla started for the kitchen.

Grampy broke that feeling. "You know, it is Christmas Eve and Chasse has a family."

"We all have our crosses to bear," Darla wasn't in the mood.

"And some of us our bears to cross," her father-in-law could be just as insolent as Dana. Well, worse. He was mother proof.

"I work, old man," Darla professed as if that was the point of contention. "All you do is sit in front of that TV all day."

"Doesn't work so well if I sit behind it," Grampy grinned.

Darla had no time for the old man and his nonsense. It's Dan's father, she thought. Dan can deal with him. Darla went into the kitchen where she found Dan wearing the ugliest possible Christmas sweater ever designed by a fashion school dropout.

He was clanging around a steaming pot and a counter of mugs, cans, boxes, spilled sprinkles and a ripped open bag of marshmallows. It looked like a lab experiment gone horribly wrong.

"What do you think you are doing?" she asked as pleasantly as she was going to.

"Special Christmas cocoa for our special Christmas guest and anybody else who wants it." Dan was thoroughly delighted when Darla had told him about Candice Siwel. She knew he would be. Dan loved kids. He would have a ball team of them if he could. So feeding them sugar before bed time, not a surprise.

"Looks like a mess, Dan," Darla was thinking about the cleanup that would come after he was done playing and who would be saddled with it.

"Darn it, Darla," Dan said, "It's Christmas cocoa. Want some?"

With Darla's help or insistence, Dan moved his center of operations to the breakfast nook where he was setting up a tray of cocoa fixings on the dinette table when Debbie bounded down the stairs and across the great room to his side.

"Daddy, the Harpy called," Debbie was loud enough to have been heard from the top landing.

"Didn't Chasse take any calls?" Darla's rhetorical question of the day.

"What could that Harpy want now?" Dan's not so rhetorical question of the day.

"She wants you to call her," Debbie yelled.

"Go. I'll finish this," Darla tried to gently pry the utensils from Dan.

"I'm not calling her," Dan had a death grip on the ladle. "It's Christmas Eve."

"Doesn't matter," Darla said. "She's your boss."

That was that. Dan exploded. "She's a four alarm migraine that has been shrieking in my ear all day. And darn it, Darla, the only reason she's my boss is…" Darla and Debbie parroted Dan even as he said it: "She stole my promotion."

Dan quieted down. "Make fun all you want," he said, "but it's true."

"It's been over a year, Dan," Darla was all about moving on. "Let it go."

"She stole it, Darla, and I'm done with the little harpy."

Debbie only read between the lines when her name was on one. Otherwise, she wasn't interested. "She said you better call her, Daddy."

"It could actually be important, Dan," Darla tried once more.

"Darn it, Darla!" Dan repeated for the last time, "It's Christmas Eve! And nothing is more important than Christmas cocoa!" He was looking over his tray of fixings. "Hey, got any whipped cream?"

"Maybe Cool Whip." Darla sighed and headed for the kitchen. Sure, she might scold, disagree or even argue with him but Dan was right. In the end, it was all about the Christmas cocoa.

Leaned back in his overstuffed easy chair, Grampy heard something that made him look across the great room to the entry foyer. There he saw the coat closet door open a crack as a pile of things tried to push their way out. An instant later, Dawnet came prancing out as Dotty squeezed out behind him. She pushed the door closed as she shoved the falling contents back inside. Dawnet sat watching, his stout little tail wagging in total contentment of a job well done. He like this game of find-the-Christmas-squirrel. Dotty made a check in her notebook and skipped over to Grampy. Dawnet was right behind her, tail wagging like a flaxen tornado.

"Ready, Grampy?" Dotty bounced up on his chair arm.

"Sure, Kiddo," he said. "Just watching *Bonanza, The Lost Episodes*."

"How can you be watching them if they're lost?" Dotty asked.

Grampy laughed as he clicked off the TV. "They just call them *The Lost Episodes* because if they called them *Bonanza, the Episodes without Hoss*, nobody would watch."

Seemed like a reasonable answer. Dotty ran her finger down her notebook page. "Dawnet and me already searched the linen closet, all the bedrooms, bathrooms, the hall closets and the coat closet. All's left is Daddy's study, the attic and the garage."

"You've been working," Grampy said with absolute admiration. "We best start with your Dad's study while he's busy making cocoa."

Grampy pushed to his feet and followed as Dotty and Dawnet pranced through the breakfast nook to the downstairs hallway. In the breakfast nook, Darla was now back with the whip cream, performing triage on Dan's Christmas Cocoa.

"Hot chocolate, Little Dot?" Dan was filling mugs.

"In a bit, Daddy," she wobbled her pencil in passing. "Grampy and I are testing a theory."

Neither Debbie, Darla nor Dan asked what theory. It never occurred to them. They were having too much fun filling their mugs and then themselves with nice warm Christmas cocoa.

Chapter 12:

When One Door Closes

Hot chocolate with a touch of vanilla bean wafted from the breakfast nook into the great room mixing with the smell of Juniper and the glowing embers in the fireplace, enveloping the entire house in a warm, peaceful holiday cheer. Then the doorbell rang.

Debbie rocketed from her chair at the dinette table and yanked the front door open.

A freezing Malynda Piper jumped the threshold and slammed the door shut with Debbie still hanging on the knob.

Debbie shouted, "Daddy, the Harpy's here!"

"Merry Christmas, Miss Piper!" Darla called from the breakfast nook, without even bothering to look.

Dan didn't handle it nearly as well. He reached critical mass faster than ground zero at Los Alamos. Ears lit and teeth clenched, Dan rushed into the great room. "Malynda, what are you doing here?"

"You wouldn't return my calls, Dan," Malynda slinked into the great room with all the grace befitting any reptile.

"Darn it, Malynda!" Dan said. "It's Christmas Eve! Did you notice, when I left, we were the only ones in the whole department? Well, not counting Zwang."

"I noticed, when you left, I was the only one in the whole department. I never count Zwang." Malynda set her snow damp briefcase on the coffee table.

"Cupcake," Dan said to Debbie, "Go have some Christmas cocoa."

Debbie was gone in a blink.

"I need a campaign for the next quarter,." Malynda began unbuttoning her coat.

"Tonight? No one will even look at it before January."

Malynda handed Dan her coat. "Ezra and Saul will. They want it now, Dan."

"Then go write it now," Dan shoved her coat back at her. "It's your job." He picked up the dripping briefcase and flung it on her coat.

"Pu-lease. You've composed the last three." Malynda dropped her briefcase on a stand by the foyer and piled her coat on top. "You have to do this one too."

"Those were supposed to be collaborations." Dan picked up Malynda's coat and held it open for her to put on.

"It was." Malynda said in mock astonishment. "You drafted it. I presented it." Malynda stepped away from Dan and the opened coat.

"You took full credit!" Dan chased after her.

"The nature of collaborations, Dan. For some reason they thought I wrote them."

"You took my name off the plans, Malynda." Dan tossed her coat at her. It fell on the floor.

"I may have done a little editing."

"You took my name off all three plans!"

"Got me promoted," she snorted as she plopped on the sofa.

"To my job," Dan snapped. "Each time, you promised me."

"Each time, you believed me," Malynda sneered. "That's not my fault."

"Doesn't it bother you that you are where you are by taking credit for someone else's work?" Dan's entire face was hot pink now.

"We were collaborating." Malynda enjoyed Dan's attempt at anger management.

"That's not collaborating, Malynda," Dan snarled. "That is stealing."

"Outside corporate, it's stealing," she said. "Inside corporate, it's appropriating resources, showing initiative, innovative adaptation, assertive omission, prevaricating."

"You mean lying!" Dan bit each word.

"Tomato, Tamatah," Malynda crinkled her nose.

"You know what they call it when you deal from the bottom?"

"Depends on your bottom," Malynda leaned back on hers. "Now Dan, we have this discussion every day and it doesn't matter. You trash me around the office every day and that doesn't matter. Like it or not, I am the PM. Like it or not, I need a theme, a promo, a campaign, something. And like it or not, I need it tonight."

Dan picked up Malynda's coat and presented it to her again. "Then go write it tonight and write it somewhere else."

"I'm delegating," Malynda oozed obnoxiousness.

"Delegate somewhere else, darn it," Dan was close to a growl now. "It's Christmas Eve."

Malynda realized a different tact was required. Something with the undertone of threat. "We are a toy company, Dan. Our slowest quarter comes right after Christmas. A lot of budgeting, cutbacks and layoffs. It is not an appropriate time to be obstinate and uncooperative if you want to keep your job. Do you want to keep your job, Dan?" Malynda held a blank CD in Dan's boiling face, a glint of cruelty sparkling in her eyes. She knew she had him.

Dan released her coat and reluctantly took the CD. "This could take a while."

"I'll wait," Malynda couldn't resist. "Just don't make me wait long. It is, after all, Christmas Eve."

The eruption was over. Malynda collected her coat and briefcase while Dan headed directly for the downstairs study. He didn't even notice Grampy, Dotty and Dawnet passing him in the hall on their way to the garage. None of them were interested in Christmas cocoa. Darla asked Debbie to see if the girls upstairs would be interested.

Debbie gulped down her cup and galloped through the living room, bouncing off Malynda and up the stairs too fast to matter to anybody accept Dan's boss who ricocheted off Debbie back on the sofa then rebounded onto the carpet.

Feeling like a pinball, Malynda picked herself up, then her coat, then her briefcase and limped over to the coat closet by the foyer. She figured why not put them away since she would be at the Oglesby home for at least awhile. The Harpy opened the closet door.

In a cacophony of muffled clangs and crashes, an avalanche of things commonly consigned to the dark recesses of a closet poured over Malynda Piper, knocking her to the floor again. Refugees from infomercials and bargain bins past coalesced in a pile of miscellaneous rinky-dinks in the middle of the foyer. Malynda lay beneath the heap on the cold wet tiles as tracked in snow water soaked through her pant suit. Icy sludge stung her where bruises on her hip and arm were already forming. She didn't melt like most witches do when they get wet. She just lay there, wondering if she could sue.

Chapter 13:

The Upside of Zero

From the breakfast nook, Darla heard the noise in the foyer and came running. She grabbed Malynda's exposed hand and pulled her from beneath the closet rubble.

"A little Christmas cocoa, Miss Piper?" Darla asked cheerfully.

In no time at all, Darla had the closet gizmos back in their cage and Malynda Piper's coat put away on a hanger. Malynda herself was swaddled in a beach towel drying by the fire.

There was an unobtrusive knock at the front door. Darla nearly took it for the house settling when the knock came again. She opened the door. Arnold Ogden Grubb Junior, or Grubworm as Dana and Dotty liked to call him, barreled in. Half frozen in a not nearly warm enough school letter jacket and shaking off snow like a wet dog sheds water, he looked more pathetic than anything else. Now understand, Grubworm had a much warmer hooded puffer coat he could have worn. The letter jacket was a hand-me-down from his older brother. He preferred to wear it no matter what because he thought it made him look cool. In truth, no jacket ever created could do that. So there was Arnold in the Oglesby foyer, trembling violently, blowing into his hands and rubbing his nose and ears in a desperate effort to ward off frostbite. A wet dog would have looked cooler. And there was Darla like a three ball juggler handling six balls getting tossed a seventh. The seventh ball being Arnold.

"Arnold," Darla had to ask, "what are you doing out and in that jacket? You could freeze in this weather!"

"I'm too tough to freeze, Mrs. Oglesby," Grubworm clattered with all the conviction of a sinner being passed the bag at a snake handling revival. "I don't even mind the snow." Anyway, that's what it sounded like he said. He was shaking so badly, Darla couldn't be sure as he sidestepped past her to the great room in a dead heat for the stairs. He would have made it too. But Grubworm stopped when he saw their Christmas tree and detoured toward it. When he pivoted back, Darla who had followed from the foyer was now directly between him and the balusters.

"What are you doing here on Christmas Eve?" Darla asked as Malynda stood up along side her, completely blocking his way to the stairs.

Without thinking, which was how Grubworm liked to do things, he replied, "I've got to see Dana, Mrs. Oglesby."

"Dana?" Darla stopped him. "I thought you were Debbie's little friend?"

Arnold Ogden Grubb Jr. was the first boy to ever look at Debbie so naturally Debbie fell madly and passionately in love with him. But then everything that girl did, she did madly and passionately. And because she was also fiercely loyal, she had continued to love Arnold, no matter what kind of jacket he wore. She was more than willing to overlook his lack of social skills (he had zero), his popularity (zero there also) and his inability to think on his feet or anywhere else for that matter.

Now Arnold had a problem. No one was supposed to know he was there to see Dana. He had to cover up his big goof. Looking as mature as he could in a ball cap and ridiculously oversized letter jacket, he said, "Oh, I was Debbie's boy friend but I'm trading up." Grubworm made a break for the stairs, trampling Malynda. Unfortunately for him, Candy, Dana and especially Debbie were at the top of those stairs and had heard everything.

"You and Arnold!" Debbie stared at her sister in shock.

"Me and Grubworm?" Dana sputtered in just as much shock as Debbie, "Not now. Not ever. Never, Deb. Never."

With Dana at the top of the stairs and her mother at the bottom, Arnold in the middle continued the charade like he might get away with it. "There's my girl!" he called out. "Hi, Dana!" The copious amounts of cheap spice cologne he drenched himself in mixed with questionable hygiene proceeded Arnold to the top of the landing.

"Dana, you're boy friend is really aromatic!" Candy choked out trying to be polite. She had to turn away. Her eyes and nose were watering from the onslaught and this was a girl who had smelled some terrible things in her life.

"Shuckydern, Dana!" cried Debbie. "I was waiting all day!"

Dana tried to calm her, "If he were the last guy on earth, Deb, I swear I'd become an astronaut."

Reaching through the haze of spice flavored B.O, Arnold tossed an arm around Dana. "Your dreamboat has come in." He saw Debbie's face and froze.

"Shuckydern! You were my dreamboat!" A tearful Debbie charged down the stairs, passed her mom, knocking Malynda aside. Before anyone could say anything, she disappeared into the downstairs hallway beyond the breakfast nook.

"You are such an idiot," Dana whispered to Arnold.

"What's wrong with Debbie?" asked Candy. "Do I have hallowed toezies?"

"No, Candy," replied Dana. "It's Grubworm's hallowed toezies. Go have some cocoa."

Candy bobbed downstairs as Dana ripped Grubworm's arm off of her, grabbed fistfuls of his jacket and a little neck as well then drug him from the landing.

Dana chewed his ear. "Grubworm, are you nuts?"

Grubworm whined like a pup, "It's your mom. What could I do?"

"Lie!" snarled Dana.

"I did," he cried.

"About who you're here to see, idiot."

Malynda joined Darla at the bottom of the stairs. They couldn't hear the actual conversation, but they could tell none of it sounded friendly. Darla leaned on the stair railing and called up to her daughter, "Dana, Arnold is here to see you?"

Dana drug Arnold back to the landing in a death clamp.

"Yeah, Mom," Dana called down with all the sincerity of a political ad. "We're an item. I know

Grubworm is short and stinky but I figure once you're passed the smell…"

"Dana, he's your sister's little friend and he is way too young for you!"

"You're right, Mom," Dana shouted. "I'll break up with him right now!"

"You can break up just like that?" Darla yelled.

"I'm very fickle, Mom!" Dana shook her little prisoner by the scruff, "Come on, Grubworm!"

As soon as they were off the landing, Dana exchanged her neck hold for a headlock and lugged Arnold down the hall to her bedroom.

Malynda Piper became a touch sentimental. "I was the exact same way when I was her age."

"That's reassuring," Darla was not at all reassured. In truth, she was more concerned than ever. Dana was a lot of things but she hoped she was not another Malynda Piper.

Still, it was Christmas Eve. Darla led Malynda to the breakfast nook where she fixed Candice Siwel and Malynda Piper the Oglesby version of Christmas cocoa.

Upstairs, Marmalade had just settled down to a long winter's nap under Dana's bed when the racket started. From the banging and yelling, it seemed clear that Dana was going to kill the little pungent male she had dragged into her lair and wasn't going to be particularly quiet about it. Humans were seldom very quiet about anything. Marmalade had already fled the other two bedrooms because of the noise. Now she had to slip out of this one as well. The Honey brown tabby could not go to the parents' bedroom because the door was closed. Darla started keeping that door closed when Dawnet joined the family. That silly dog did not even know how to use a litter box. And still, they kept him! At any rate, Marmalade could not go downstairs because strangers were there. She could not stay upstairs because there was a noisy murder being committed. Absolutely no choices. That's why the cat hated this holiday. In a corner of the landing under the railing festooned with an evergreen garland of silver bells, Marmalade curled up behind a stuffed Santa Doll decoration and fell asleep.

Chapter 14:

The Downside of Zero

Dan was in his study clattering furiously on his computer keyboard when a single loud knock struck his door. Before Dan could say anything, before he could do anything, before he could even look up, the door popped open and Debbie ran in, crying fiercely. She slammed the door and plowed into him still sitting in his chair at the roll top desk. Dan put his arms around his little girl as she sobbed uncontrollably into his shoulder.

"Cupcake, what happened?" he asked.

"Dana stole Arnold, Daddy." Debbie's voice was muffled in his shirt.

"Dana and Arnold?" Dan thought he must be misunderstanding.

"Uh-huh," her voice quivered between sobs. "After I waited for him too."

"Darn it, Debbie!" Dan said softly. "That can't be right."

"I know," Debbie agreed. "It's so wrong but there they were, making out in front of Mom."

"Nothing about that sounds even remotely right." Dan wasn't just comforting his daughter either. Dan knew there was just no way anyone in that family besides Debbie would ever go for Grubworm and no way any of his daughters would ever make out in front of their mother —ever. Not even Dana. He was pretty sure, anyway.

Certainly not with Grubworm. The only redeeming quality the kid had was he would always run at the first sight of Dan. Then again, the boy ran from everybody. Good instincts. It was only a matter of time before some other kid decked him. Dan wouldn't be surprised if there was a line forming. Grubworm was one of those boys who spent recess dodging bullies and super wedgies while trying futilely to raise his social standing to something above zero. He was just incredibly lucky to have stumbled into a relationship with a cute girl like Debbie and entirely too self-absorbed to appreciate it. Typical teen. But luck alone couldn't get a punching bag like Grubworm to the tenth round without a beatdown. The kid needed to find himself before somebody else did and that didn't look likely.

"I waited for him all day, Daddy," Debbie was soaking Dan's shirt with tears.

"You shouldn't have to wait for any boy," Dan told her. "He should be waiting for you. Besides, Arnold smells."

"Arnold does not smell!" Even broken hearted, Debbie was as loyal as ever.

"Debbie, someday your allergies are going to clear up and, what I mean is, someday, you may feel differently."

"You mean," Debbie was working up to another round of tears, "I'll feel even worse?"

"No Cupcake. I mean things are going to turn out for the best."

"Huh? How do you know?"

"Because you deserve nothing less," Dan kissed her on her cheek.

Still teary, Debbie smiled. That's why she came to him. Daddy could always make every end of the world crisis Debbie faced seem more like a bad moment. And not even all that bad.

In the safe harbor of her dad's arms, she rested the side of her head against his chest when her eyes wondered to his PC screen. Stick figure drawings and mundane clip art surrounded a litany of cliches so bad they would make any corporate mission statement read like something by Irving Berlin.

Arnold completely forgotten, Debbie sat up and stared in astonishment at the screen.

"It's for the Harpy," her father beamed.

"Like one of those?" Debbie pointed at stacks of CDs in the pigeon holes of his roll top desk.

"Oh no, Cupcake. Those are all award winning campaigns. This is the worst I've ever written. In fact, if I do it right, maybe the worst campaign in the history of advertising."

"You're doing this to hurt the Harpy?" Debbie squinted at the screen.

"She is a Harpy." Dan felt that justified the lot.

"Nice people don't do things like that on Christmas Eve," Debbie shook her head as if she could shake what she was seeing out of it.

"They do to Harpies." Dan simpered.

Debbie stared in disbelief at her father. He was the good guy, she thought. "Not even to Harpies."

"I didn't start this. I'm finishing it." Even as he said it, Dan realized how wrong it seemed. Still, it was for Malynda Piper, the Harpy of all Harpies.

He set Debbie on her feet and walked her to the door. "Now go help your mother or something so I can get this done."

Debbie was already racing down the hall when Dan shouted, "And don't worry about Arnold, Cupcake!"

Chapter 15:

The Suppository of All Knowledge

In the breakfast nook, Candy and Malynda were seated at the table with their own cups of cocoa, a tray of baklava and a half dozen holiday mugs. Darla was pouring some for herself when Debbie bolted out of the hall, across the nook and into the great room. By the time Malynda and Candy looked up, Debbie was gone.

In the corner of the great room by the foyer, Debbie pounced on the landline and dialed the number on Johnetta Hoyle's business card crumpled in her hand. As the receiver trilled in her ear, Debbie mumbled, "I didn't start this. I'm finishing it."

Back in the nook, Malynda was trying to clean up her brand a little for Darla. "You know, I'm not a monster," Malynda said with all the candor a monster could muster.

"Dan has never called you a monster," Darla was busy doctoring her cup.

"He certainly acts like it," Malynda found that being a persecuted woman generally played well with other women. She didn't factor in that Darla happened to be in love with the man she was attempting to paint as her persecutor.

"Dan has called you a lot of things, Miss Piper," Darla replied, "but never a monster." Technically, Harpies were only mythical monsters, not actual living monsters. Right?

"Just 'Malynda' please," Malynda was striving for personable. "It's a little unfair of him to make my promotion the great disapprobation in his life. It was an opportunity and I took it. Like he would. Like anyone would. I have a career too."

"He did take it a little too personal," Darla said hoping to satisfy Malynda Piper and end this conversation. She took her cup and headed for the great room to put a little distance between herself and Dan's boss so maybe, just maybe, she would not have to listen to Malynda anymore. There was something creepy about Malynda's voice when she was trying to sound affable —like getting nuzzled by a shark. Candy followed Darla for the same reason. Any other rattlesnake would have sat there happily coiled around its cocoa. Not Malynda Piper. She followed them both and did not shut up.

"Some men cannot accept being beaten by a woman," Malynda was about to regale them with a blow by blow of how she cleaned Dan's clock.

"Dan wasn't feeling beaten, Malynda." Darla was done. She seated herself on the far end of the sofa, Candy nested in the middle and Malynda seized the near end.

"Of course, I don't mean I beat him," Malynda did an about-face. "Simply that he might look at it that way."

Candy barged in on Malynda Piper's second stab at character assassination. She took a deep sip and whispered, "Thank you Mrs. Oglesby. I really depreciate hot cocoa."

Darla laughed. "My pleasure, Candy!" Then in a long breath to Malynda, "Dan didn't look at it that way. He was expecting that promotion for a long time. He planned for it. He dreamed about it. When he didn't get it, well, he didn't get it."

As any decent propagandist knows, not every lie stands up. Malynda instinctually knew there needed to be a redirection of the conversation or it would not end well for her. "Ah, now that is Christmas in a cup," Malynda said without taking a single sip. "So how's your work? Book keeper, isn't it?"

"CPA. Well, accountant now. CPA someday."

"Someday?" Malynda acted surprised which was impossible since she didn't care. "You haven't made CPA yet?"

"Family first, career second," Darla said.

"Anything else first makes you second," Malynda sensed a new soft spot to drive a wedge in. "And nobody remembers who came in second."

"I don't want to be remembered, Malynda," Darla began to strain, weary from the wearing. "I just want a good job."

"Only two jobs in the jungle, Darla: Eat or get eaten. The rules to survival are simple: Don't get eaten and eat as much as you can." Malynda loved sharing her insights for two reasons: One, it didn't take long because she didn't have that many. And Two, it didn't help either. Just made her look smart.

"I suppose it is dog eat dog out there," Darla was agreeing with Malynda the way a sane person agrees with any axe welding lunatic. Smiling and nodding while looking for an exit.

Candy on the other hand viewed axe welding lunatics differently. "Catatonically, you should eat all things in modern-nation."

"Don't interrupt," Malynda blustered. "When you are an executive as I am, then, maybe, someone will want to hear your inane observations. Until then, keep your mouth shut." In the Paper, Rock, Scissors world of idioms, Malynda didn't like being upstaged by anyone, especially some teenager.

"Oh," Candy looked down, a little tremble in her voice, "So you're like the suppository of all knowledge?"

"Not like it, Candy," Darla laughed. "She definitely is." Darla looked over at Candy and winked. Candy smiled at Darla and winked back. Oh, the power of big words.

Grampy, Dotty and Dawnet had come in quietly from the garage. Dotty and Dawnet stopped in the breakfast nook for cocoa while Grampy went straight to his easy chair. A tousled Chasse had just made her way down the stairs.

"It wasn't just the linen closet," Chasse was reporting to Darla but glaring at Dotty through the doorway to the breakfast nook. "A tiny tornado blew through the whole place up there. It's straightened out now."

"You think upstairs was bad," Dotty spoke in gulps of hot chocolate, "you should see the attic."

"What were you two doing in the attic?" Darla apparently knew who the local cyclone was.

"No worse than the garage," Grampy was more concerned with finding Bonanza on the TV than the state of the Oglesby household.

"What were you two doing in the garage?" Darla stared at the old man.

"Going to the attic," replied Grampy. "Are you not listening?"

"Again, what were you two doing in the attic?"

"Testing my theory, Mommy." Dotty bubbled just like it explained everything.

"Mrs. Oglesby," Chasse hoped she had done enough for this woman, "I have to catch my bus.."

"First check the garage and attic, Chasse," Darla did not want to contend with any extra old messes. There would be plenty of new ones tomorrow.

"But Mrs. Oglesby…" Chasse was pleading now.

Darla cut her off. "It will only take a moment." Of course, it was not going to only take a moment or Darla would have done it herself.

Chasse realized that no amount of hurrying was going to get her to the bus stop on time and resigned herself to a long walk home in the snow. She hoped her kids could find something in the refrigerator. Nothing worse than a hungry child on Christmas Eve.

In the garage, a spring ladder hung down from the open trapdoor to the attic. It seemed like both vehicles were awash in tools, old sporting goods, yard games and the remains of a rummage sale. But it wasn't that bad. A few boxes needed to be stacked and one of the cabinet doors was ajar from a few out of place whatsis but, all in all, Chasse made quick work of the space and mounted the ladder.

It was the attic that had been turned upside down and given a shake. It was almost as bad as Dotty's room. Chasse looked over the debris field up there and decided the fastest course of action was to put like with like in separate piles. It wouldn't be really cleaned up in any way but it was all junk and junk in piles looks better than junk all over. Regardless, it would still be junk. And so much of it! The only two real solutions would involve moving or arson. Nobody in that household would go for either so piles it was.

Fully recharged by her cup of Christmas cocoa, Dotty skipped over to Grampy's chair. Without a thought, Candy put her empty cup on one of the dozens of coasters Darla had distributed throughout the house and climbed over Malynda taking out a couple of toes on her way to join Dotty. Grampy was just back to watching Bonanza when he found himself surrounded by girls.

"I would love to hear your hypotenuse, Dotty," Candy dropped to the floor beside Grampy's chair. Dawnet plopped under the footrest on his back for his usual perspective. That was a dangerous place for a little dog if the person in the recliner sat up suddenly. Since it was Grampy, Dawnet was perfectly safe. The old man did nothing suddenly.

"It's not important, Candy. I was wrong." Dotty took her usual place on the arm of the easy chair.

"Don't be sad, Dotty," Candy whispered. "I'm wrong all the time except when I'm right."

"What now, Kiddo?" asked Grampy.

"I don't know, Grampy. We looked everywhere and no presents," Dotty frowned.

"Or we just think we looked everywhere," Grampy put an arm around his little granddaughter.

"We did, Grampy!" Dotty went over the search in her mind. "Everywhere! No presents. No conspiracy."

Grampy nodded in sympathy. "Then we're back to Santa covering the earth in one night and that's not likely."

"If only we had an eye witness account," Dotty's head rested in both her hands now, "but no one has ever actually seen Santa delivering presents."

"Clement Moore saw Santa deliver presents," Candy said ever softly.

"Who?" Dotty wasn't even sure if she heard the name right.

"Clement Moore," Candy answered enthusiastically. "He wrote *A Visit from St. Nicholas*."

"That's just a poem," Dotty sounded skeptical.

Candy was not the least bit discouraged. "One place I stayed, they read it every Christmas like a true-diction or something. Maybe it was just a poem, but it sure sounded like Mr. Moore saw something."

Dotty's whole face lit up in a sudden realization. "Candy," she cried, "you're so smart!" Dotty leaped from the chair arm and hit the floor running. Dawnet rolled to his feet and was at her heels. In a second, she was squatted in front of one of their two bookcases framing the fireplace. Dawnet sat beside her, ever on guard for mailmen, newspapers, that cat and now the Christmas Squirrel. In another second, she had a book of children poems in her arms and a minute later was open to the poem, *A Visit From St. Nicholas*.

Candy leaned over and whispered to Grampy "Squeak! She thinks I'm smart!"

Grampy whispered back, "Life makes you smart until you are. You've had more than your share of pain. You're bound to have more than your share of wisdom. These girls have more than their share of happiness. Maybe if you share your gift with them, they'll share their gift with you, Princess."

Candy smiled. He called her 'Princess'. Grampy knew!

Chapter 16:

A Fistful of Collar

Providence is the wine of the weary. Darla could have used a little Providence as Malynda prattled on. "Now where were we?" Malynda was preparing to launch into yet another soliloquy. "Talking about me or how to become me?" It was then, the doorbell rang. "Someone's at the door?" Malynda couldn't believe it. At this hour? On Christmas Eve? Who would do such a thing? Besides her, that is.

Darla on the other hand knew whoever was on the other side of that door had to be better than Malynda. She was as much running from Malynda as she was running to the front door. It didn't matter. Malynda stuck to her like a wet tongue on frozen metal —but not nearly as pleasant. Darla barely turned the knob when Johnetta Hoyle pushed in, a cloud of fog and snow trailing after.

Johnetta charged from the foyer into the great Room, rolling over Malynda Piper who recoiled in horror though you would think she would be used to being trampled by now. Johnetta Hoyle didn't care. She was on the prod, excited by the hunt. As she gabbled on, Johnetta waved both arms so violently and wildly that had she done so simultaneously in the same direction, she would have probably taken flight.

The most Darla got from it was that the Pod Pirate was Dana or Grubworm or both and the proof was here right now. Ms. Hoyle knew it because somebody just called to tell her so. Darla waited for Johnetta to stop flapping. It didn't take long. She tired easily.

Darla approached the bottom of the stairs and called out in her stern mother voice, "Dana Oglesby! Arnold Ogden Grub Junior! Get down here! Now!"

Dana and Grubworm appeared on the top landing. Dana had just stuffed a ten dollar bill from

Grubworm into her hip pocket. Grubworm was still holding the CD she gave him without stuffing it anywhere. Dana grabbed Grubworm by the scruff of the neck and towed him in her wake as she casually popped downstairs. Dana thought this was still about her courting Debbie's little darling. "It's okay, Mom," Dana said. "I'm throwing the little perch back."

Johnetta Hoyle began waving and pointing frantically. "See! See in his hand! In his hand!"

Grubworm was mystified for a second before he realized she was talking about the CD he just paid ten dollars for. Like an inflatable spaghetti armed air dancer, Grubworm flailed around helplessly in Dana's grasp for nearly a full minute before it occurred to him he should probably hide the CD.

Dana only smiled. "Ms. Hoyle? Thought you were gone for the Holidays!"

The doorbell rang again.

Malynda had just regained her footing. "Now who can that be?"

"Oh, the police!" Johnetta Hoyle turned for the front door, trampling Malynda yet again.

"The police?" Darla repeated in disbelief.

"The police?" Malynda echoed as she banged into something.

"The police!" Grubworm cried in full panic. He could not wriggle free of Dana's grip on his collar. There was no place to run anyway though Grubworm hadn't thought that far ahead.

"It wouldn't be the Holidays without the police," Dana said, as if she were commenting on snowmen, nutcrackers or mistletoe.

Grampy witnessed the entire drama from his easy chair, checked his watch, then slipped away. Candy leaped into his chair before a blaring TV as Johnetta opened the front door. Looking like he got dressed in a blender, a dog tired David Caldwell stumbled in from the storm. Johnetta led him to the great room and introduced him as "Detective David Caldwell of our fair city's police department, here to enforce my citizen's arrest."

Caldwell wasn't really there to enforce anything or arrest anyone. He was there to keep Ms. Hoyle happy. "Merry Christmas," he said as his eyes gauged the room. That's when they locked on Dana Oglesby and her eyes locked on him.

Quickly Dana pulled the big clip from her hair and finger combed her locks around her shoulders. Grubworm gawked at her, dumbfounded. He never knew Dana to care about her appearance before. She cared now and it didn't matter. To David Caldwell, Dana was a green eyed beauty.

To Dana, Detective Caldwell was Humphrey Bogart, Robert Mitchum and Steve McQueen stuffed into one heavy trench coat and wool fedora. In truth, he was just a very tired young man who could have used a shave, a bath and maybe four or five hours sleep.

Darla tried to get her daughter's attention. "Dana, Johnetta Hoyle thinks you're the Pod Pirate and you've sold one of those evil video games to Arnold."

Dana's voice went up half an octave and pretentiously respectful. "Where would she get a silly idea like that, Mother?" Darla was surprised into silence. This was not her daughter. "I mean, really Ms. Hoyle, you drag this poor man out into the cold on Christmas Eve away from his wife."

"Oh, I'm not married," said Caldwell.

"Or his girlfriend," continued Dana.

"I don't have a girlfriend," said Caldwell.

"Really Detective Caldwell? You know I'm a high school graduate, legal age and everything,"

"Everything?"

"The complete package," It was like they were the only two in the room. They weren't. The others were just dumbfounded.

"Oh my God," thought Darla. "She's flirting!"

"The boy has the CD, Detective," Johnetta stabbed her pointed finger at the air in front of the terrified Grubworm so harshly, he flinched. "I saw him hide it!"

Not exactly hide. Grubworm shoved the CD in his hand into one of the letter Jacket's side pockets. Nevertheless, Grubworm squirmed like a young bourgeoisie on his way to the guillotine.

Dana remained calmly amused. She stuffed her hand into his pocket and pulled the CD easily from Grubworm's death grip. "As it happens," she smiled at the detective, "I did sell him this CD."

"She confessed! She's the Pod Pirate! It's one of those satanic games!" Johnetta spit hysterically.

"Let's put it in a PC and find out?" Dana waved the CD casually in front of the socialite's nose.

Johnetta snatched it from her fingers. "Not in your PC!"

Darla snatched it from Johnetta. "There's one in the kitchen." She headed there. Johnetta followed with Malynda Piper. Dana, grappling Grubworm with one hand, put her other arm in Caldwell's arm and they strolled together. Debbie popped up from behind the sofa and trailed after them.

Leading the parade to the kitchen, Darla caught Grampy in the breakfast nook rummaging through her purse. Everyone was surprised except Darla. She just seemed mildly annoyed. "What are you doing now, Grampy Coy?"

Grampy didn't seem surprised either. "A little pilfering," he said and pocketed some bills.

"Well, pilfer somewhere else." Darla snatched her purse and shooed him away then continued through the saloon doors to the kitchen. Her entourage filed pass Grampy as he headed to the great Room and the telephone.

Darla walked over to a small PC on the kitchen island counter and shoved in the CD. Malynda, Johnetta, Debbie, Dana and David Caldwell crowded around. There was a momentary whirling as the CD loaded. Grubworm looked at his shoes. Dana and David stared dreamily at each other. Everyone else watched the PC screen.

A silver mist appeared on the screen then slowly lifted to reveal a beautiful flower garden in intricate detail right down to the stamen. Moving deeper and darker into the little garden, the player perspective drifted over leaves, petals and vines until it stopped at a small wooden door, barely big enough for a bunny. A little sign on the door read "Tap Twice for your Fairy Fantasy". Everyone was blown away by the beautiful graphics.

"Something isn't right," Johnetta grabbed Grubworm from Dana. She shoved him at the PC. "Boy, play the game!"

Grubworm reluctantly climbed on the swivel stool. Looking straight down at his lap, he double clicked the mouse. A Blue window appeared flashing: Enter Passcode.

"Passcode? What's a Passcode?" Johnetta squawked.

"Some security thing," Dana sighed. "Just hit enter, Grubworm."

As soon as Grubworm tapped the enter key, the door swung open and beautiful little fairies started prancing around the garden waving their wands in a sparkle of fairy dust. Whenever the fairy dust touched a plant, flowers budded and bloomed. The object was to keep the flowers watered with an on-screen watering can. Sounded easy but in no time at all, Grubworm was behind and flowers faded in tinkling bells then floated to Heaven on harp music.

"You can see why a boy might be a little embarrassed about a game like this but it really is fun." Dana smiled at David who was smiling back.

"That is cute," Darla's interpretation of the 'Aws' and 'Oohs' coming from everyone else.

"No little boy wants to be caught with cute, Mom," Dana was Dana again, all the time making goo-goo eyes at the detective.

Grubworm in the midst of serious game play felt the need to point out, "It's a stocking stuffer for my big brother. Honestly. It's not for me."

"See?" Dana said. "Even now he won't admit it. Didn't even want Debbie to know."

"Shuckydern!" Debbie cried. "I thought Dana was stealing Arnold from me. I called Ms. Hoyle."

Darla, Malynda and Johnetta Hoyle gaped at Debbie. Grubworm was too busy with the game and Dana was too busy with David Caldwell.

"Course you did," Dana was not the least upset. "See, Ms. Hoyle. Just a case of a woman scorned."

"You aren't the Pod Pirate?" Johnetta was devastated.

Dana smiled up at Detective Caldwell. "Not tonight," she said.

Tears were rolling down Debbie's cheeks. "I'm so sorry, Ms. Hoyle. I was waiting all day to hear from Arnold." She frogged Arnold's arm. "I was waiting all day to hear from you!" Arnold only yelped. The fairy game required all his brain power. "When he did show up, he asked for Dana. Not me. I waited all day, Ms. Hoyle. All day!"

"Why did you call me and tell me your sister was the Pod Pirate?" Johnetta asked.

Debbie cast her eyes on the floor in unequivocal shame. "I had your business card."

"You're really not the Pod Pirate?" Johnetta looked wistfully at Dana.

"No Ms. Hoyle," Dana pressed a little closer to the Detective. "Just your normal, sweet, available girl of legal age."

"The complete package," Caldwell added.

"So David," Dana asked, "you work every holiday or just Christmas?"

"Usually just Christmas," Caldwell said.

"Why? Were you a naughty boy?" Dana teased.

"No," Caldwell chuckled. "Me and some of the other single guys volunteer for extra shifts so the married guys can spend a little more of the holiday with their families."

"Aw, that's so sweet," Dana was touched.

"You haven't seen their families," Caldwell replied. Dana giggled.

"So you could go to the New Year's Ball?" Dana scrounged a pad and pen from a drawer.

"Isn't it too late to get tickets?" Caldwell was a little puzzled. Dana scribbled furiously.

"My Grampy can get tickets," Dana tore off the page and stuffed it in the Detective's coat pocket.

"Really?" Caldwell watched her fingers jam in the paper.

"My Grampy's got peeps."

Darla couldn't help but be a little suspicious. "Something about all of this doesn't make sense."

"Oh please, Mom," Dana was almost too quick. "Grubworm's an idiot, Deb dropped a dime on me and the smart detective has figured it all out."

Suddenly Caldwell realized it had been a full day since he slept. "I think we've interrupted this family's Christmas long enough, Ms. Hoyle."

"You don't want to arrest me?" Dana embraced the young detective.

"Maybe not arrest you…" Caldwell had arms around her too.

"Question me then? You should really question me," Dana was never sweeter.

"What about her?" Johnetta inserted her face between them and punched a pudgy finger at Debbie. "Making a false charge!"

Caldwell was unfazed. "She didn't call the police, Ms. Hoyle. You did."

"Oh," Johnetta reversed. "But I didn't mean it."

"Neither did she," he said. Teary eyed Debbie felt a little better.

Darla leaned over Arnold. "You can put your game away now, Arnold."

"I tell ya, it's a stocking stuffer for my big brother," Arnold was on automatic. The boy just made second level and wasn't stopping for anybody.

"One moment," Dana tenderly released the Detective, then put her lips by Grubworm's ear and in big sister voice, "Put it away, Grubworm!"

In one spasmodic jerk, Arnold Ogden Grubb Jr closed the app and popped the CD. He barely pocketed it when Dana clamped his collar and drug him off the stool. The group paraded out of the kitchen across the great Room towards the Foyer.

Dana locked one arm in Caldwell's. "So what about the Ball?"

"It's a lot of fun with the right person," Caldwell only had eyes for Dana.

"I could be the right person," Dana never looked more affectionate.

"I can see that."

"You can?"

"I'm a detective. We notice things."

"Not keys!" Johnetta did not forget this morning. Caldwell winced at her. "Don't worry, Detective. I'll commend you to your captain for coming out tonight. A lot of men wouldn't."

Darla couldn't help but be impressed. Mrs. Baklava was right. Johnetta Hoyle was fair after all. "I'm sorry how this all turned out, Johnetta. You should have called first before driving all the way over again on the word of a child."

"I would have, ordinarily," Johnetta replied. "It is just the call made me think. All those other little boys at the school knew Dana too. How many little boys know big girls by name?"

"As I recall," Darla said, "All of them."

At the front door, Dana dangled Grubworm at Johnetta. "Maybe you could drop Grubworm home, Ms. Hoyle. He's right on your way."

"That's alright. Really. I can walk." Grubworm squirmed, wriggling to get away.

"Not in this weather with that jacket," Dana gave him a shake. "What do you say, Ms. Hoyle?"

"Why not," Johnetta said, taking custody of Grubworm's collar as she headed out into the cold.

"I said I can walk," Grubworm pleaded. "Please God, let me walk." But God in his infinite wisdom wasn't going to let that happen.

Johnetta Hoyle marched boldly down to the street with a fist full of Arnold Ogden Grubb Junior slipping and stumbling along side her. At the jeep, she tossed him into the backseat like so much luggage, slammed the door and slogged around to the driver side.

"Merry Christmas!" She called out to the folks clustered in the Oglesby front door.

"Merry Christmas, Johnetta," Darla called back. "If there's anything I can do for you..?"

"Tear up my business cards!" Johnetta shouted and with that, she was gone.

Detective David Caldwell was next out. "I apologize for the intrusion, Mrs. Oglesby." He paused at the threshold long enough to tip his hat.

"Merry Christmas Detective," Darla said, closing the door.

"Merry Christmas!" David waved back.

"Text me!" shouted Dana as the door shut.

"Text me?" Darla did a double-take.

"Please Mom," Dana protested, "It's not like I'm Deb."

Just then, Dana caught Debbie peeking around the corner from the great room. The girl's eyes were red, her cheeks moist, her heart crushed.

Dana rushed her kid sister before she bolted, snagged her in both arms and hugged her until she stopped struggling. She pressed Debbie's head to her shoulder and kissed it gently.

"Arnold's never going to see me again, is he?" Debbie sobbed.

"Sure he will," Dana replied, consoling her. "We're not that lucky."

Chapter 17:

Santa's Big Day

While romance, confession and a game of dancing fairies was taking place in the kitchen, Grampy was on the phone to the local Taxi company.

"Yawp," he said, "I'd like a cab sent to forty two Bailey… It's a brick home like every other house on this street…Why?… Distinguishing features?… Oh, you mean, how is it different from the other houses?… Well, it has a four and a two on it…Going to tenth with one or two stops along the way… An apartment… How long? Thanks… Sure, that would be fine… Would you like the number?.. Yawp, that's it. Bye."

Grampy hung up the phone and headed back to his easy chair. Candy already plunked herself onto one chair arm. Dotty was plunked on the other, the big Illustrative Book of Children Poems in her arms. As soon as Grampy settled into his chair, Dawnet settled into his lap. Dotty opened the children's book to the poem *A Visit From St. Nicholas* and leaned it on Dawnet's back. Dawnet didn't mind. A book stand was one of his many talents.

Dotty began, "Santa is an elf, Grampy. Explains everything." Grampy Coy and Candy both looked quizzically at Dotty. She continued. "Elves don't ride rabbits and birds like fairies. They ride tiny versions of what people ride. And it says right here: 'A miniature sleigh and eight tiny reindeer'. Not a normal size sleigh; a miniature one. And not regular size reindeer; tiny ones. And elves are small, Grampy. Even a fat elf could easily slide down a six inch stove pipe."

"He doesn't look like an elf in any of these pictures," Grampy said, looking at each drawing that accompanied each verse on every page.

"Artist conception, Grampy. You have to ignore the pictures and go by what's written. That's the testimony."

"I knew Clement Moore saw something," Candy was absolutely delighted that she helped.

Dotty nodded, "He sure did, Candy. It says plain as day: 'A right jolly old elf.' Not a man, Grampy. An elf. And then this next line: 'A wink of his eye and a twist of his head soon gave me to know I had nothing to dread.' Elves use a magic stare called glamour to make people docile. And nowhere does the elf call himself St. Nicholas. Mr. Moore just assumes he is. See Back here (she flicked a couple of pages), it says: 'A little old driver so lively and quick, I knew in a moment,' he assumes, Grampy, 'it must be St. Nick'."

"Let's say Santa is an elf," Grampy said. "How does that resolve your time problem?"

"Elves manipulate time, Grampy. Rip Van Winkle took a two hour nap in an elf camp and woke up twenty Year's later. A classic case of severe time dilation. One night to us can be several years to Santa."

"Yawp. Two hours equal twenty years would make for a really big day for Santa, alright. Where did you learn so much about elves and time dilation?" Grampy asked.

"I listen to Coast to Coast AM," she replied.

"Isn't that on after your bed time?"

"Dana stream links it for me."

"Of course, she does," Grampy laughed.

The small mob that had wondered across the great room to the foyer was now diminished to a horde and making its way to the dining table. Dotty jumped from the chair arm to join them and grabbed Candy's hand. Dawnet leaped from Grampy's lap and raced ahead of everyone.

Chasse had just cleared the fixings and cups from the breakfast nook when the phone rang. This time there was no competition to answer it. The Grubworm drama was over. Chasse hurried regardless and picked up the handset. "Hello?..." She turned and saw Grampy right behind her. "Did anyone call a cab?"

"That's your cab, Chasse," Grampy said. He took the handset from her, thanked the dispatcher and hung up the phone. He pulled the roll of Darla's bills from his pocket and placed them in Chasse's hand. "This ought to cover your ride home and maybe some kind of Christmas Eve supper for those kids of yours." He walked her to the coat closet by the Foyer and helped her with her coat. "It's too late to catch a bus, Chasse. This'll have to do."

"But Mrs. Oglesby?" Chasse said weakly pulling on her coat.

"We'll tell her I sent you home. She'll be mad at me then." He opened the door for her. "Better get going before anybody notices."

"Oh, Merry Christmas, Grampy," Chasse teared up and kissed him on the cheek. Grampy turned a flustered pink as she rushed down to the cab waiting in the street.

"Something about this holiday," he mumbled as he watched the cab slowly crunch over the snow and away.

Chapter 18:

A Turkey and Some Mistletoe

Grampy barely closed the door when Beck Lovat blocked it with her shoulder draped in a thickly insulated parka. She was only slightly squished between the door and frame. "Beck!" Surprised, Grampy flung the door wide open. "Just in time for supper!"

"I've already eaten, Coy," Beck said stepping into the Foyer. "I was watching for you."

"Ah! So are you a little voyeur, stalker, busybody or just plain nosy?" Grampy closed the door.

"Just plain trying to catch up with you," she laughed.

"Then you can plain watch us eat." He took Beck's parka and hung it in the coat closet.

"I just wanted to make sure..." she began again.

"You can make all the sure you want after supper." Before she could protest, Grampy had her at the dining table.

"Have you met Malynda Piper?" he asked.

"She's a real Harpy!" For the moment, Debbie was fully recovered from Arnold. It is a special super power all young girls have.

"I'm Beck Lovat," Beck introduced herself to Malynda before anyone else could introduce her as Mrs. Baklava. "You can call me Beck."

"But we call her Mrs. Baklava," Debbie interjected. "And this is Candy."

"We call her Candy," Dotty added.

"I think we all know Candy by now," laughed Beck. "You look much warmer, dear." Beck settled in the open spot by Grampy.

Darla had just returned from talking to Dan in his study and could see everyone was already passing the turkey and all the fixings around the table. Nobody was waiting for anybody. "We're having dinner without your father tonight," she announced.

No one much noticed. Darla took her chair and joined the fray.

"I sent Chasse home," Grampy told her.

"I know," she said.

"You paid for her cab," Grampy gauged her reaction.

"I figured as much," Darla nodded.

"And Christmas Eve dinner for her kids."

"Well, I am the Queen of Nice," Darla skewed a smile at him.

"Yawp," Grampy smiled back. "Sometimes you really are."

"So Coy," Beck asked, "why doesn't your name start with a 'D'?"

"Because that's not how you spell 'Coy'," he answered.

"You know what I'm talking about. There's Dan, Darla, Dana, Debbie and Dotty. Even Dawnet. And then there's you, Coy."

"Don't forget Marmalade," shouted Dotty.

"Who's Marmalade?" asked Beck.

"She's our cat," Dotty replied.

"You have a cat?" Beck was astonished. "I've never seen a cat."

Debbie's impish grin betrayed the exaggerated spookiness in her voice. "Nobody ever does."

"Yawp. Marmalade just walked in one day and stayed," Grampy waved the words away like a fly.

"I named her," Debbie proffered. "She's the color of home made marmalade."

"And absolutely nobody tells that cat what to do either," Darla added. "She comes and goes exactly as she pleases. Just like she owns the place."

"And nobody sees her unless she wants to be seen," Grampy said, "so I'm not the only one in the house whose initials aren't D.O. I'm just the only one who gets seen."

"Truly bizarre though," Malynda scraped the ceiling with her eyes. "Everyone's name starts with a D?"

"Except the cat and Grampy," Dotty shouted.

"It's very simple," Grampy elucidated like any good liar. "My son and his wife decided to save on monogrammed luggage and towel sets; one set of initials fits all. Course, me and the cat never go anywhere."

Darla declared over the teetering, "You cannot believe anything that old man says."

Dana popped the back of her hand by her lips in an exaggerated aside to Dotty, "Told you."

"It was completely unintentional," Darla continued. "It just sort of happened. Originally, we were going to name our first born after Dan. We didn't have a boy so our first was named 'Dana'."

"Could have name me Danielle," Dana opined.

"Not your father. He was set on 'Dan'. But since you were the first and a girl, he would accept Dan-A or Dana."

"Sounds obstinate," Malynda was ever looking for that wedge.

"Obstinance is a sandwich best served plain," Candy remarked, "for condiments make hoagies of us all." Everyone laughed but Malynda.

Darla chatted on. "Debbie was named after the only snack food in the hospital vending machine the weekend I gave birth to her. Dana and Dan lived on them."

"Good times," Dana quipped.

Debbie through her head back and her arm over her eyes as she waxed melodramatic, "I was named after a cupcake."

"And just as sweet," Candy's compliment made Debbie blush a little as all the girls laughed.

Darla was ignoring the girls completely. "Dan liked the name 'Debbie' because he thought it followed some formula."

Grampy expounded on it. "His oldest was 'Dan-A' and his second was 'Deb-B'."

"How is she registered on her birth certificate?" Malynda seemed nearly interested.

"Not 'Deborah Lynn Oglesby'," Darla tapped each invisible syllable in the air in front of her as she mouthed them. "Debbie Lynn Oglesby".

"Dotty doesn't fit any of that," Beck side-eyed her in perplexed amusement.

"Dotty was named 'Dorothy' after the little girl in the Wizard of Oz. It happened to be on television the night she came into the world."

"I have the red slippers to prove it," Dotty yelled.

"We received lots of little red booties for her," Darla got a touch reminiscent.

"How about Dawnet?" asked Malynda. "Who gives a little male dog a girl's name?"

"I don't know about the sex," Beck observed, "but it is an unusual name for a dog."

"Accidental as well," Darla said. "Dan decided the girls needed a dog to learn responsibility."

Dana interrupted, "As if Marmalade didn't already teach us that. If the food or water dish was even low, somebody's shoes were getting barfed on." Both young girls nodded in agreement. "And God help you, if you didn't clean the litter box."

"We just wanted a dog, Mommy," exclaimed Dotty.

"Yeah, we just wanted a dog," agreed Debbie.

"Well, that was how your father sold it to me," Darla bowed to their version. "Whatever the reason, Dan and the girls went to the Rescue and found this little puppy that looked like the dog from the Wizard of Oz. They were going to name him 'Toto' and teach him tricks."

"Dawnet is one really smart dog," Grampy interjected.

"Well, the girls couldn't train him," Darla went on. "He made doggie deposits all over the house, tore up any shoe that crossed his line of vision and ran away anytime he could."

"Made Marmalade look pretty good," Dana frowned at her two sisters.

"He only ran away from you, Mommy," Dotty defended Dawnet but she wouldn't lie for him.

"Like I said, one really smart dog," Grampy winked at Beck.

"Dan decided it was up to him to train the dog," Darla said.

"Every day," Grampy jumped in, "Dan would spend a couple of hours in the yard with that animal trying to get him to do something, sit, stay, heel, roll over, anything on command. Every day!"

"He would get so frustrated!" Darla was laughing. "He would be standing out there shouting at the top of his lungs in that Boston accent of his…"

"Like if he was louder, maybe the dog might understand," Grampy declared.

Darla mimicked Dan's accent, "…Now sit, dawn it! Sit! Stay, dawn it! Stay! Come, dawn it! Come!" She wiped tears from her eyes, she was laughing so hard. "By the time Dan was done, both the dog and the girls firmly believed the dog's name was Dawnet." Everyone laughed as Darla added, "That dog still won't come when I call him."

"Yawp," agreed Grampy. "One really smart dog."

Dawnet sat at attention under the table at the very center of his pack where he belonged. Since Dan wasn't there, he was pack leader and the other pack members were clearly compelled to call his name and do that funny howl they call laughter, showing their great respect and admiration for him —kissing his ring, so to speak. Still, he was a little concerned. He hadn't seen that pesky cat all day.

Down from her perch on the landing, Marmalade had been skirting the edges of her downstairs territory currently invaded and occupied by outsiders. She did, of course, investigate the dining table while no one was looking. No decent cuisine. Just turkey. Poor things couldn't find anything worth eating, she mused. Just as well. The interlopers joined them. As soon as everyone cleared the great room, Marmalade vanished back upstairs to wait it out until the invaders were gone. There were some dog toys she needed to destroy anyway.

Malynda checked her watch. "Can someone look in on Dan?" she asked.

Beck didn't want to be the one holding up the family's holiday so she said her goodbyes, wished the family one more Merry Christmas and headed for the door.

Grampy volunteered to walk Beck home. He helped her with her parka, put his parka on then grabbed his personally wrapped present from under the tree. Beck and Grampy plodded through the snow from the lit porch of the Oglesby home to the lit porch of Beck Lovat's cottage next door.

"Coy, are you going with me to the ball this year?" Beck studied his poker face.

"I've gone with you every year," he said in make believe protest.

"For the last five years," she said.

"No reason this year should be any different."

"But you never ask me. I always ask you."

"Yawp. And I always go."

"You never stay over either."

"Nawp. But I always come over."

"You don't like me that much?"

"I like you fine. It's the family."

"Your family doesn't like me?"

"They like you as much as they like anybody, I expect."

"Since I've known them, I don't think one of them ever called me by my name. Not once."

"Well, that's your fault." There was a sudden twinkle in the old man's eyes.

"My fault?"

"Remember the first time you came over?" Grampy said. "You brought a tray of that baklava."

"My signature treat."

"So you told me."

"Everybody said they loved it," Beck was feeling a trifle insecure. Maybe they didn't love it. Maybe they didn't even like Baklava. Maybe they hated it.

"I know," Grampy smiled. "I wanted to find out if they really did love it or if they were just being nice. A lot of times, they're just being nice."

"What's that got to do with my name?"

"I told the girls if they ever hoped to see any more of those treats, they should know you prefer to be called 'Mrs. Baklava'. Turns out they really love those things. Turns out everybody in the family really loves those things. Even Chasse really loves those things." Beck blinked in wide eyed astonishment. It should have occurred to her this was one of Coy Oglesby's jokes; this one lasting almost seven years.

They were at the front door of Beck's cottage. She fumbled with the lock.

"Then why can't you stay over, Coy?"

"As hard as it is to believe, the Oglesby Clan couldn't make it a day without me."

"I don't believe they really feel that way," Beck tiptoed tactfully around the fact that, aside from his two youngest granddaughters, nobody over there seemed to take Grampy seriously ever. They stomped the snow off their boots and went in.

"Oh, I know they don't think so," Grampy beamed proudly, "but a lot of times, I'm the only common sense they got. They think I'm dead weight but I'm the anchor of that family."

"Well, if you ever need to come ashore," Beck said, "you can dock here."

Coy laughed. "I know and I'm grateful, but I got to take care of those kids."

"There does seem to be a lot going on over there now."

"Oh, there's always a lot going on over there. That's what makes it fun."

They stopped beneath the mistletoe hanging from the living-room header.

"Merry Christmas," Grampy said and handed Beck her present, possibly the ugliest wrapped gift to ever grace a Christmas tree. Hand printed on a beautiful attached card: 'To Rebecca Lovat from the Oglesby Clan. Thank you, Mrs. Baklava.'

"Oh Coy," Beck melted like ice cream on hot blueberry cobbler and kissed him.

"Something about this Holiday," Grampy thought and kissed her back.

Chapter 19:

Don't You Tell A Single Soul

Supper was done and the Oglesby kids were getting antsy. With Grampy next door, the channel changer was up for grabs. "I wonder what Christmas Specials are on," Dotty said, instigating the stampede.

"Hold it," shouted Darla, de-instigating the stampede. "Clear the table first."

Candy immediately jumped to her feet and happily started collecting plates. "I can clear the table, Mrs. Oglesby."

"Yeah," agreed Dana. "She can clear the table, Mom."

"You can all clear the table," Darla wasn't about to impose work on a guest.

"But it would be my gift to your family," Candy rounded up the plates and silverware.

"It would be her gift, Mom," Dana said.

"You really don't mind, Candy?" Darla asked.

"I would be absotively deluded to do it, Mrs. Oglesby," Candy chimed, a stack of dishes already in her hands.

"She would be absotively deluded, Mommy," said Debbie.

"Absotively deluded," repeated Dana.

"Well..," Darla waffled only a moment and the stampede was re-instigated.

Malynda Piper sat watching while Candy and Darla cleared the table. She did not move. She did not offer to help. She was a PM for goodness sakes. Darla and Candy both were "absotively deluded" she didn't help. At last, they were away from her. In the kitchen, Candy scraped plates and loaded the dishwasher while Darla fixed a plate for Dan and warmed it in the oven.

In the great room, Debbie and Dotty were in a tug of war for the channel changer. Dawnet skidded around the room, barking joyfully. Keep-away was a game he understood. Dana hovered over them like a pool player studying her shot. Then with surgical skill that only comes from years of experience wrestling things from your sisters, Dana snatched the channel changer effortlessly from their grasp. Both girls flailing around her, Dana clicked on the TV as she plunged into the sofa. Dotty shrugged and plopped on the arm of Grampy's Easy chair. Dawnet jumped up on the cushion beside her. Debbie was not nearly so philosophical. She stood there, hands on her hips, glaring at Dana who grinned at her as she clicked through channels.

Dan finally appeared from the downstairs hallway. The dining table looked like the aftermath of a locust plague. He flicked the CD into Malynda's lap. She picked it up. "It's about time, Dan," her words soothing as a broken jar of scorpions. "See me to the door?" Malynda slithered triumphantly through the great room. Dan followed.

"One fully detailed Campaign?" Malynda asked as they reached the foyer.

"Want to look it over?" Dan collected her coat and briefcase from the closet. Malynda slid the CD into her briefcase as Dan held her coat open for her.

"I trust you," she slipped into her coat then fingered through her briefcase.

"And this is a little something for you." Malynda pulled out the big grey envelope and handed it to Dan. "Better update your resumé, Dan. You're fired."

Dan stared at the envelope in disbelief. "I'm worth any two admen in the whole company, darn it!"

Malynda's smirk showed how much she enjoyed this. "True," she said, "but I can hire three of those admen for what I pay you."

"Who's going to write your next campaign?"

"Who cares?" Malynda's eyes narrowed. "I'll make Staff VP before end of next quarter. And if I get my wish, by next Christmas, I won't be worrying about promos, car payments, rent or nothing."

Dan's anger boiled up in his throat and choked him. "You kept me late when everybody else left early. You ate dinner with my family while I wrote your stupid campaign. And on Christmas Eve, darn it! How can you go home and sleep tonight?"

"I've had a big dinner." Malynda looked up and saw the mistletoe hanging with two silver bell decorations from the center of the foyer. Her lips spread into an alligator grin. She coiled her arms around Dan and gave him a big wet kiss. "Merry Christmas, Dan," Malynda croaked and rushed out the door. Dan turned to see Debbie less than one step away staring in abject horror. He had no idea how long she had been there. As it happened, not long.

Debbie was still fuming over Dana stealing the channel changer when she saw Dan and Malynda heading for the foyer. She was certain that once she told her Dad how Dana stole the channel changer, he would, of course, take her side. She hesitated a moment or two because she was pretty sure bothering Daddy while he was talking to a business associate was wrong. But, she rationalized, controlling the channel changer was far more important so Debbie darted full gallop for the Foyer. She only arrived in time to see Malynda kissing Dan full on the lips.

Dan thought Debbie heard Malynda firing him. "What did you hear? What did you see?" Instantly, Dan's red face turned an ashen white.

"Nothing, Daddy. Nothing." Debbie knew immediately she must have seen something she wasn't supposed to.

Dan grabbed the teenager by both arms and pulled her close to his face. "Don't say anything to your mother, understand? Not a word, darn it!"

Debbie could see Malynda's mauve lipstick smeared across her Daddy's face. "Not a word, Daddy!" She shuddered. "I promise."

Dan saw in his panic he had unintentionally scared his little girl. He released her. "I'm sorry, Cupcake," Dan said, stroking her hair. "Daddy had a bad day." Debbie only nodded. She didn't know what to do. She never seen her father act like this before. "Go play or something," Dan said. Debbie shot out of there. Who had the channel changer did not seem so important anymore.

Darla watched from the breakfast nook as Debbie ran to her sanctuary behind the sofa. Dana was sprawled across the entire sofa, clutching the channel changer. Dotty was balanced on her favorite arm of Grampy's chair. Both were watching television and laughing. Debbie stared at the TV alright but was undeniably troubled. Then Darla saw Dan wiping his mouth as he walked quietly from the Foyer to the breakfast nook. Darla had a warm plate of turkey and trimmings waiting for Dan when he sat down at the table. Darla watched Dan stare at his dinner with the same despondency Debbie was showing for the TV. "What's the matter, Dan?"

"Some people in this world are pure evil," was all he said.

Darla looked out into the great room at Debbie on the verge of tears. "You didn't take Malynda Piper out on our Little Dee, did you?" Dan only glowered at his plate. "I don't know what all you're getting for Christmas, Dan, but I know what you're NOT getting tonight." With all the enthusiasm of a vegetarian at a Texas chili cookout, Dan poked his turkey with a fork. "When you're done, make sure the girls go up." Darla could see Dan was more troubled than angry. "Better eat before it gets cold," she said and kissed him on the neck.

Chapter 20:

Everybody Believes in Somebody

For a child, a year is an eternity —long enough for the old, tired reruns of Christmas to seem all new and wonderful again. Dotty was well into it. Dana wasn't because she was no longer a child but she had the channel changer and that was good enough. Debbie should have been into it but she couldn't be. She knew what she knew when she knew it and that ruined Christmas for her. Naturally, she had to share it with her sisters and ruin Christmas for them too. "Dana! Dotty!" she whispered —sort of. She drowned out the TV.

"I'm keeping the channel changer," Dana declared, more in the fun of pressing her sister's buttons than the buttons on the channel changer.

"Forget the channel changer. Forget Christmas. Daddy's having an affair with the Harpy."

"Miss Piper?" Dotty couldn't believe it. Daddy was too perfect to do something like that.

Dana saw their mother coming and immediately shushed her sisters.

Darla kissed Dana on her forehead. "Goodnight, Big Dee," Darla said.

"Goodnight, Mom," Dana replied.

Darla kissed Dotty on her cheek. "Goodnight baby," Darla said.

"Goodnight, Mommy." Dotty answered.

Finally, Darla kissed Debbie on her cheek. "Goodnight, Little Dee," Darla said.

"Goodnight Mommy," Debbie answered.

Then Darla knew. "What's going on?"

All three girls replied, "Nothing, Mom."

Darla eyed them all suspiciously. "Something's going on." The girls avoided eye contact. "Whatever this little drama is," Darla warned, "I want it done by bedtime."

All three nodded in unison. "Okay, Mom!"

It was clear they weren't going to talk. Darla headed upstairs. "I mean it," she yelled from the top landing. "I am the queen of bedtime."

The girls' heads followed their mom up the stairs and off the landing. They remained craned and silent until they heard the distant click of Mom's bedroom door latch. All three snapped around!

"How do you know?" Dana was not one to jump to conclusions. She would rather walk to them.

Already primed, Debbie exploded. "The Harpy hugged him, then she kissed him then he made me promise not to tell."

"That can't be," Dotty was plainly upset. "We didn't ask for that."

Both Dana and Debbie stared at their kid sister like she had three heads.

"The silver bell," Dotty explained.

"That's just a kid game," Dana said.

"Shut up, Dana. You don't know," Dotty scolded. "Mommy and Daddy and us, we're going to do things together and Daddy is going to be home more and…and…"

"Dad is going to appreciate the great genius that I am?" Dana had faith the way some folks have pizza. Free delivery only and without anchovies.

"Whatever. From our lips to God's ear," Dotty sniped.

"Maybe God didn't listen," Dana suggested.

"Or maybe we made God mad." Debbie's comment quieted the other two. They remembered what Candy said. God didn't like to be tested.

Grampy was just back from Beck Lovat's place next door. He was putting his Parka in the Foyer closet when Candy skipped into the great room.

"Okey Dokey, guys," Candy spoke almost normally as she dropped beside Grampy's chair. "Dishes all done. What are we watching?"

"Candy," Dana asked. "Who was Mr. Rolle?"

"The guy who knew it wouldn't snow Christmas," Candy replied.

"I mean, what did he do for a living?" Dana pressed gently.

"Oh," Candy answered cheerfully. "He delivered newspapers."

"The paper boy?" Dana looked askance at Debbie then Dotty.

"How old was Mr. Rolle, Candy?" Debbie leaned over the couch.

Candy noticed nothing. "Twelve, I think," she said. "He could have been younger."

"Shuckydern!" Debbie gasped. Unquestionable certainty had turned to definite doubt.

Dotty did what many folks do when their dream dies. She attacked the most vulnerable one near her. "Candy, you're about the stupidest person in the world!" Candy was shocked and bewildered.

"Go to bed, Candy," Dana put it like an order, not a request.

Candy fled up the stairs to Dotty's room. She dropped on her knees and fished her little Silver Bell ornament from it's sacred place in her handbag. Tears poured down both cheeks as she quietly held the bell to her quivering lips, cupped her hand around the rim and whispered, "Please, God. Squeak! Please make Dotty think I'm smart again." She returned the Silver Bell to her purse, wiped the tears from her cheeks and eyes, pulled a blanket down from the top of the bed then curled up on the cold floor beside it.

Marmalade happen to be under that bed, contemplating which of the dog's toys she should destroy tonight. The cat immediately sensed the little human was upset and frightened. Probably the silly dog's fault. Marmalade would have to fix things — as usual. The honey brown tabby quietly eased up to Candy's neck and sniffed her ear.

Candy turned her face toward the cat. "You must be Marmalade," she choked out softly between tears and gently stroked her fur.

Marmalade pushed herself under the blanket and snuggled against Candy's warm body. She rubbed her chin and whiskers against the girl's face as cats sometimes do.

Cuddling the purring tabby, Candy kissed the top of the little cat's head, "You know how to treat a Nubian Princess," she whispered soft as a cat's whisker then drifted off to a peaceful sleep.

"Anyone tries to hurt you now will have to answer to me," the cat thought. Naturally, Marmalade took the first watch.

Grampy was standing in the Foyer when Candy ran upstairs in tears. He could see Dan in the dining area staring at his supper and the siblings sibilating in front of the TV. "I can't leave this family alone for five minutes," he thought and walked over to his chair.

"Okay, girls, what's going on?" Grampy slowly parked himself into the hidy-hole pocket of his recliner. Dawnet leaped into Dotty's lap.

"Daddy loves the Harpy," Debbie couldn't have sounded more heartbroken.

"What makes you think that?" Grampy couldn't have sounded more incredulous.

"Debbie saw Malynda Piper kiss Daddy." Tears tugged at Dotty's voice.

"Doesn't mean a thing," Grampy threw an arm around Dotty in a way that made her sure everything was really alright. "I myself have been getting kissed right and left all day. It's something to do with the Holiday."

"But Daddy told me not to tell Mom," Debbie dropped beside the old man's knee.

Grampy whisked away a tear escaping down her face and tugged playfully at her chin. "Little Dee, if I got kissed by Malynda Piper, I wouldn't want anybody to know either."

Still on the sofa, Dana tilted over the end closest to the recliner. The old man was a grand-daughter magnet. "Mom went to bed early, Grampy. She only does that when she's really mad at Dad."

"That doesn't mean he's messing around," Grampy said. "Just off the top of my head, I can think of a dozen good reasons to be mad at your father at any given moment and none of them have a thing to do with Malynda Piper."

Dana was not quite convinced. "Regardless, if Dad leaves Mom, I'm moving in with Dad."

"But Daddy's never home," Dotty fussed.

"Exactly," replied Dana.

"Nobody's leaving anybody," Grampy said.

"How can you be so sure?" Debbie wanted to believe. She needed to believe.

"Little Dee, you've seen your mother and you've seen Malynda Piper. If you were your father, who would you pick?"

"Nice one, Grampy. Hard to argue with logic like that." Dana leaned back again.

"But shuckydern! She kissed him, Grampy." Debbie saw what she saw when she saw it.

Grampy remained unruffled. "I didn't say Miss Piper couldn't have a lapse of judgement. Heck, even your mom married him. But between your mom and Miss Piper, it seems to me, your Dad has a much easier choice."

"Yeah," agreed Dana. "No guy would take Malynda Piper over Mom."

"Well, something happened," Debbie said. "Her lipstick was all over him."

"Something probably did happen but not what you think," Grampy stroked her hair.

"How can you be so sure?" asked Dotty.

"Yeah, old man," Dana piled on. "How can you be so sure?"

"Debbie thought you were making out with Grubworm earlier," Grampy playfully whacked the bottom of one of Dana's dirty pink fuzzies.

"So I'm wrong?" Debbie prickled.

"There's nothing wrong with you, Little Dee," Grampy leaned back in his chair. "You're just a hundred percent heart at a hundred miles an hour. You're bound to run off the road once in a while."

"Gees, Grampy!" Dana replied. "Wrong is wrong."

Both her sisters cried together: "Shut up, Dana! You don't know!" Then Debbie asked him, "How can we find out what really happened?"

"You let me worry about that," Grampy winked. "You kids need to worry about getting to bed."

"Its not a school night," Dotty protested.

"Nawp. It's a Santa night," Grampy said. "You proved that, kiddo. He could be here any minute."

Debbie and Dotty jumped to their feet as Dana clicked off the TV and dropped the channel changer.

Dumped from Dotty's lap, Dawnet recovered mid fall and rolled behind the recliner, barely dodging Dana's dirty pink dust mops scooshing the carpet.

Leaning over, Dana hugged her Grandfather. "Someday, this is all going to catch up with you, old man," she kissed him on the cheek. "Goodnight, Grampy."

"Goodnight Trouble." Dana made for the stairs.

The other two tag-teamed him, both hugging and kissing him from both sides. As soon as they said their goodnights, Debbie had already shot passed Dana on her way up the stairs. Grampy stopped Dotty. "You weren't very kind to our little guest."

"I didn't tell her anything she didn't already know," Dotty looked down. She knew better.

"You want her to stay away from you?" Grampy asked.

"No."

"When you hurt people, that's what they do. They stay away. Believe me. I know. I've done it myself too many times." Grampy spoke softly.

"She admits she doesn't know anything, Grampy. She says it all the time."

Grampy turned Dotty's face toward his. "Seems to me, Kiddo, a person who admits they don't know much is a lot smarter than someone who thinks they know everything."

"Okay, Grampy," Dotty said. "I'm sorry."

"Nothing to apologize to me for," Grampy told her. "But one thing I learned is this: Everybody knows something but nobody knows everything. Sooner or later, we all need help from somebody. So you should treat everybody like they're that somebody because you never know who your somebody is going to be. It could be Candy."

"Oh," Dotty knew Grampy was right. Candy had already helped with her Santa problem. More importantly, Candy had been nothing but kind.

"I'll go tell her I'm sorry right now," Dotty thought she should fix this before Santa arrived. She didn't want to end up on the naughty list.

"No, Little Dot. You let Candy sleep. But next time, you want to tell somebody something, ask yourself if it's something you would want them to tell you. If it's not, chances are they don't need to hear it from you either."

"I will, Grampy."

"Now go to bed so I can get some sleep."

Dotty kissed and hugged him again and said "I love you, Grampy." A second later, she was bobbing up the stairs, all the night's drama completely forgotten. She had barely reached the landing when Dawnet shot up the stairs from his hiding place behind the recliner, his tail wagging so fiercely it seemed to propel him that much faster.

Grampy was not so fast. He was barely on his feet when Dana hurried down the stairs with a little present wrapped in white brocade and tied with a large blue ribbon and bow. "What kind of mischief are you up to now?" He watched her set it on the popcorn tin.

"I thought it would be nice to have something extra under the tree for Candy," Dana said.

"What is it or do I even want to know?" Grampy asked.

"My little Princess hair brush Mom and Dad got me for my Sweet Sixteen. I never used it. Way too Gucci."

"You think Candy will like it?"

Dana grinned at her Grandfather, "Oh, she's gonna love it. Nighty-Night Old Man!"

"Goodnight, Trouble." Grampy smiled as he watched Dana disappear up the stairs. There were moments when she was his favorite. This was one of them. He saw Dan brooding in the breakfast nook and walked over. Dan hadn't touched a thing.

"Girls are mad at me, huh?" Dan moved the food around his plate.

"Not especially. Not tonight. But all your kids hate you one time or another," Grampy snatched a roll off his plate. "You get used to it."

"Don't want them to hate me at Christmas," Dan sighed.

"A father's job isn't to make his kids like him. It's to do what's best for them. The rest will work itself out," Grampy smiled at his son.

Dan stood up. "I better get the presents down while I can hold my eyes open."

"Oh, they're not in the study closet anymore," Grampy said. "I had to move them to my room."

Dan and his father lumbered through the downstairs hallway to Grampy's bedroom, collected the kids' presents and placed them around the tree. It took two trips. Dan was carefully arranging the gifts around the tree. To marketing guys, presentation is everything.

She still believes in Santa?" Dan asked.

"She still believes in me," Grampy said and headed for bed.

Chapter 21:

The Happy Dog

Early Christmas morning, the windows were so frosted over, you couldn't see it not snow. Grampy was already up, fully dressed and starting his second pot of coffee. It was only an eight cup pot, after all. He had dutifully turned on the Christmas lights so they would greet the girls when they crawled out of bed and came down. Dawnet was already on his back deep beneath the underbelly of the Christmas tree, staring at that accursed golden ribbon. Tail curled around all four paws, Marmalade sat calmly on the handrail of the landing where she could keep an eye on both the bedroom hallway off the landing and the great room below. The impending deluge of gift wrap wouldn't start until the first squeal.

The squeal never came. There was no ribbon strewn heaps of discarded gift wrap surrounding a cornucopia of store bought delights. No usual testament to childhood avarice where children learn the anticipation is always better than the outcome, the fantasy is always better than the fact and the dream is always better than the drivel. Important lessons softened by a series of little surprises and a sugar high to be forgotten in a few weeks and relearned again next year. But not this morning. There were no girls.

Only Dana. She shuffled down in her robe and dirty pink fuzzies, uncombed hair clipped to the top of her head, laptop in hand and plopped on the sofa. Then Dan and Darla in their robes and slippers.

It was Darla who spoke first. "Where are they?"

It was Dana who answered. "I'm here."

"Not you," Dan was sleepwalking to the breakfast nook following the scent of freshly brewed coffee. "Where are they, Dad?"

"Still nestled down snug in their beds, I imagine." Grampy himself nestled down snug into the overstuffed comfort of his recliner.

"I don't blame them," Darla was right behind Dan. "The Grinch had nothing on you last night."

Since Grampy was busy searching for his channel changer, Dawnet still burrowed under a pile of gifts, Dan picking out a couple of Christmas mugs for Darla and his coffee and Darla blaming Dan for anything and everything that went wrong this Christmas (it was practically a Holiday tradition with her), only Marmalade saw Debbie and Dotty quietly coming down the stairs.

"Sorry," Dan said to Darla's amazement. Usually there was a little resistance before he took full responsibility. "I didn't want to ruin everybody's Christmas."

"So far, your plan has worked brilliantly." Grampy always encouraged his son, no matter how much it demoralized him.

"Malynda fired me last night," Dan fluttered two fingers at the Foyer. "Right there beneath the mistletoe."

Dotty and Debbie leaped down the stairs, across the room and slammed their father in little girl bear hugs of love or relief or maybe both. Darla was only three feet from him and they beat her. Didn't matter. Darla threw her arms around the rest of him.

Dana didn't move from the sofa but she was plenty mad. "After making you do her homework? We got to nail her, Dad."

"I almost did." Dan confessed. "She took full credit for the last three campaigns I put together. I figured she would do the same this time so I wrote the most moronic campaign I could think of."

"You spent all evening writing a bad promo?" Darla couldn't believe that was possible.

"Surprisingly, it's a lot harder than you think,"

"Is that why she fired you?" Darla couldn't imagine someone just firing her Dan either.

"She didn't even look at the plan," Dan wobbled like a bauble-head. "She wouldn't know a bad campaign from a good one anyway. I think she wanted everyone to believe beyond all doubt that this campaign was one hundred percent hers so she fired me."

"And it's an idiotic promo?" chirped Dana. "Nice one, Dad."

"Yawp," Grampy was feeling under the seat cushion now for his missing channel changer. "I expect her removal from Hamelin toys will probably set some sort of land speed record."

"Wow, Dad. You're pretty glib for a guy who just lost his meal ticket," Dan said.

"I can always stay with your brother, Frank," Grampy was practically upside down in his chair.

"Frank? He won't even visit since you moved in." Not that Frank ever visited in the first place. It was a private joke between Dan and his father and was bound to get trotted out during the holiday.

"And you've never thanked me," Grampy's expected response. Frank never visited. That was true. But he would always call every holiday, usually late in the afternoon. Frank, Grampy and Dan would poke fun at each other for about two hours before hanging up to do it again the next holiday.

It was Darla who noticed. "You said you 'almost did', Dan?"

"Someone who I deeply respect told me nice people don't do things like that on Christmas Eve —not even to Harpies." Debbie knew her Daddy was talking about her and gave him an extra warm hug.

"So what did you give Malynda?" Darla asked.

"A copy of the best campaign I've ever written. Hamelin will be able to adapt it easily to any of their product line."

"Marvelous," Grampy was clearly distracted. "Has anybody seen the channel changer?"

"Great," Dana was back to fuming and tapping her key board furiously. "So it's up to me to defend the family honor."

"You'll do no such thing, young lady!" Darla was adamant.

"But Mom!" Dana pleaded. For all her bravado, Dana was in truth her Dad's greatest fan.

"Dana," Darla cut her off, "if Malynda Piper is the type of person Hamelin Toys wants, they deserve her and they sure don't deserve your father."

Being a mother, Darla always preferred reasoning with her children before actually murdering them.

"What a sweet thing to say," Dan looked into Darla's eyes.

"I'm the Queen of Sweet," Darla barely got it out before Dan kissed her deeply.

"I must be adopted," Dana couldn't mask her utter revulsion at what she considered a completely contemptible act on the part of her parents —kissing right there in front of everybody, meaning Dana. Nobody wants to see that. Just knowing they did it was bad enough.

Dotty was more of a pragmatist. "Are we going to lose our home and everything?"

"We're not going to lose anything, Kiddo," Grampy grumbled from upside down in his recliner, "except maybe the channel changer."

"What makes you say that, Dad?" Dan had just resigned himself to being middle aged with a family, a mortgage, two car payments and no job.

"Because I can't find the darn thing," Grampy was trying to look under the chair now without getting out of his seat. Not easy.

"Not the channel changer; the house," Dan said.

Grampy collapsed back in his chair and drew a deep breath. "I believe everybody in this family tells me the truth."

"Isn't Bonanza on somewhere?" Darla's furtive attempt to distract the old man.

"Can't find the channel changer," Grampy answered with some annoyance. "How many here have heard Dan go on and on about how he carries Hamelin Toys very near single handedly? Show of hands." Everyone but Dan raised a hand. "Ought to be a lot easier now when all you have to carry is yourself."

"You are not suggesting I start a business out of this house?" Dan couldn't help but be skeptical. His father was a man who knew more about lobster traps and baseball than he did running any business.

"Do it on the internet," Grampy replied. "According to Dana, a website is like having a little shop on the world's busiest street corner. You're bound to get a little foot traffic. Salesman like you ought to do fine."

"You don't just open a website, Dad," Dan said. "You have to have graphics, data security, a payment system. You need a web master, darn it."

Grampy pointed at the sofa. "You got one of those right over there. Show them your handiwork, Dana."

"Grampy," Dana was probably miffed though it was exceedingly difficult to distinguish that from her normal curmudgeonliness. "You promised not to rat me out!"

"And you promised to stop all that bootlegging game silliness. Now show your parents."

With the exception of Grampy, the entire family collected behind the sofa and peered over Dana's shoulder at her laptop as she started the Fairy Garden game of beautiful flowers and pretty fairies dancing around them. In the center of the screen, the blue box appeared flashing PASSCODE. Darla applauded, "Oh, the cute little fairy garden from yesterday. Those are yours?"

Dana smirked at her mom, "Watch what happens when I enter the passcode: GRUBWORM."

In one click of the enter key, the little idyllic garden was replaced with an apocalyptic desert world of skeletal buildings and burning tires. The fairies morphed into flesh eating zombies with armored motorcycles and jeep like rock crawlers. Shrieks of terror, explosions and machine gun fire exploded from the laptop's micro-speaker. Body parts and blood were spattered across the streets and buildings. Debbie gasped in horror as Darla and Dan quickly averted Dotty's eyes. Somewhere in all of this, Dana felt the channel changer stuffed between the cushions of the couch, pulled it out and tossed it to Grampy who immediately turned on the television —his idea of holiday cheer.

"I started password protecting and encrypting stuff after that kid brought one of my little applications to school and almost got me nailed," Dana was already up to the third level of the game.

"That's some of the most realistic carnage I've ever even seen on a video game," Dan said.

"It's the blood that does it, Dad," Dana manipulated the controls like a maestro directs an ensemble. "Most people work on color but you got to have that texture and flow right to make it really work."

"You are so sick," Darla was still in shock.

"Please Mom," Dana seemed barely focused on the game. "I just design what little boys want. They're the pervs. Not me."

That's when it dawned on Debbie. "You are the Pod Pirate!"

"Yeah, Deb," Dana laughed. She was on the fourth level now. "The only time in your whole life you ever lied, you still told the truth. I have got to be adopted."

"Thing is," Grampy was clicking through the channels, "if Dana can do those kind of graphics, she can design anything you need."

"You're the one who hacked into all those professionally designed games at school?" Darla was just connecting the dots herself. That's what happens early morning when you don't get coffee.

"Yawp," Grampy nodded.

Dana corrected him. "To be clear, I didn't do that. It was my script alright, but I didn't infect the school library with it. I wouldn't be that stupid. Some little doofus thought it would be funny."

"And it hasn't happened since," Grampy noted proudly, "Means she can probably make a pretty darn secure website."

"And I want to do this because…" Dana terminated her game and stared at the old man.

"Because you get to play with your computer all day, help your family, finally have a job that's more fun than waiting tables and maybe, just maybe avoid serving time."

"Serving time? Really, Grampy?" Dana made a face at the Old Man.

"Could happen if that Detective Cobweb calls again."

"Caldwell, Grampy. Detective David Caldwell. And he will come by, won't he?"

"Of course, he will, Trouble. He's not blind." That made Dana smile.

"I have to admit," Dan patted Dana's shoulder, "you're better than the best at Hamelin. I'd say pure Genius, Big Dee."

Darla gaped at Grampy. "You knew she was Mobius Dick, the Pod Pirate?"

"Me and every twelve year old in the county," Grampy squished a grin at her.

"I can't start a business without product," Dan could turn pebbles into boulders when he wanted.

Grampy clicked off the TV in frustration. "I bet there's a sack load of little toy makers out there with a sack load of toys and no way to market. Sell their stuff."

"Still need a research lab, Dad."

"What research? I can't count the number of times I've seen you bring home some fully researched thingamajig or gizmo just to ask the girls what they think."

"Sure Dad. Those were toys and these are children. Children know toys."

"Yawp. So skip the lab coats and go straight to the source. The girls won't mind helping." That's all Grampy had to say to start the younger sisters jumping up and down and jabbering excitedly. Debbie was sure she could run the toys by the kids at school. Dotty was already planning her survey forms, charts and analysis reports.

Even Dawnet crawled out from under the Christmas tree to join in the fracas. He didn't know about reports but he understood joy perfectly.

"There's still legal and all those financials," Dan was barely audible above his kids and barking dog.

"Son," Grampy was losing patience. "You're married to the best CPA in the County, maybe the whole State." That was when Darla pried herself from Dan, rushed to Grampy's chair and gave the old man his first Christmas kiss right there on his cheek.

Grampy blushed a little and mumbled, "Something about this holiday."

Dan only got within arm's reach of hugging the old man when Grampy pushed a hand in his face. "So much as try to kiss me, I'll deck you where you stand." Dan laughed.

Dana who had been quietly tapping on her laptop announced, "I got the name of our website, DO-DADS. DO is our initials D.O. and you're our Dad so DAD. We're going to sell all sorts of little toys, gadgets and trinkets or doodads so DO-DADS. Give me a minute. I'll have our trademark and icon.

"Darn it, Dad," Dan was overwhelmed. "I think this will actually work."

"Marvelous," Grampy was relieved. "Now if you don't mind, my Bonanza marathon is on." Grampy dropped back in his recliner, pointed his channel changer at the TV and just like that, he was off on the Ponderosa.

"All he ever does is sit in front of that TV all day," Darla said, shaking her head.

Dan nodded in agreement. "I love him too."

Chapter 22:

The Bell Curve

It was Dotty who first realized that all three of their wishes to the Silver Bell had just come true. Their Dad would be spending much more time at home, they would be doing things as a family now and Daddy even recognized his oldest daughter as a genius. Just one day ago, none of that seemed remotely possible. And now, it was impossible to imagine it any other way. From their lips to God's ear. The Silver Bell worked!

Dana was not so convinced. After all, there were silver bells without clappers all over the city, probably all over the world. If silver bells really worked like that, there should have been wishes granted all over the place. From everyone's lips to God's ear. Why should Candy's bell ornament be so special? Dotty and Debbie agreed but thought maybe wishes were indeed granted all over the place on this and every Christmas. Everyone was just so busy being happy, they didn't notice. Or as her sisters put it: "Shut up Dana! You don't know!"

The girls were still chattering about it when a sleepy eyed Candy shambled down the stairs. They ran to her.

Dotty and Debbie each took one of Candy's hands and pulled her towards the tree. "Merry Christmas, Candy!" they shouted laughing.

"You guys not mad at me no more?" Candy was astonished.

"Mad at you? For what?" Debbie had completely forgotten last night.

"For being stupid." Candy had not.

"You're not stupid, Candy," Dotty remembered what her Grampy told her. "I have it on the best authority, you're about the smartest person in the whole world!"

Both girls laughed as Candy did a tiny squeak of joy. Candy's Christmas wish had indeed come true.

No surprise. Candy's Christmas wish always came true.

It wasn't ten minutes before the great room became awash in ribbon strewn heaps of discarded gift wrap surrounding a cornucopia of store bought delights. And noise. Lots of noise. There was squealing, laughing and joyful confabulation in a rambunctious celebration of each other. It should have been yet another lesson in fancy versus fact. But it wasn't. Nothing from the underbelly of that Christmas tree compared to those four little wishes already fulfilled. Nothing.

Until the phone rang.

Chapter 23:

Nor Doth He Sleep

The Employee parking lot was empty at Hamelin Toys when a dark sedan trundled over the snow to the passenger drop-off zone directly in front of the main entrance. The bright morning sun had cleared most of the frost from the glass walls of the lobby but done nothing about the snow covered ground. Cloaked like the grim reaper, Malynda Piper crawled out of the sedan and crunched across the snow crusted forecourt to the lobby door. She used her card key to gain entry. And again, at the elevator. It wasn't long after, Malynda walked the silver bell lined corridor to the CEO suite and deposited her Dan Oglesby CD into the mail-drop on the office door. The door swung open immediately and Ezra's head popped out.

"Malynda!" he exclaimed. "What an unexpected pleasure!" Ezra retrieved the CD before Malynda finished jumping out of her skin. Grinning broadly, he motioned for Malynda to follow him. "Our new promo? Come in. Come in. Let's have a look."

She followed obediently. Malynda was too startled to say or do anything else. She hadn't expected to see anyone. Saul was at his desk as usual, glasses precariously balanced on the tip of his nose, still preoccupied with his computer. Ezra sprinted to his own seat and excitedly shoved the CD into his PC. Malynda took the only chair in front of Saul's desk.

As usual, Saul didn't look up. "So Malynda, in on Christmas?"

"She brought the new marketing plan," Ezra chortled, waiting for it to come up.

"Don't you guys take Christmas off?" Malynda had counted on being in and out of an empty building today, not making nice with the head honchos.

"We're Jewish, Malynda. We don't actually take Christmas off," said Ezra.

"We don't actually take most holidays off," said Saul.

"At least sleep in?" Malynda did not understand how anyone who could not be fired wouldn't take full advantage of a holiday. She certainly would.

"You wouldn't catch God sleeping in and he's God," said Ezra.

"Universe can't run itself and neither can our little toy company," said Saul.

"We like most holidays though," said Ezra.

"We especially like Christmas," said Saul.

"We love Christmas," said Ezra.

"If it wasn't for Christmas, we wouldn't have those wonderful songs," said Saul.

"We wouldn't have those wonderful toys," said Ezra.

"We wouldn't have this wonderful business selling those wonderful toys while listening to those wonderful songs," said Saul.

"You know, Christmas was started by a Jew," said Ezra.

"A rabbi, I think," said Saul.

"Wonderful holiday," said Ezra.

"Mazel Tov," Malynda needed them to stop before her head exploded. Blessing them usually worked. Not this morning.

"I wasn't sure you'd come in today," said Ezra.

"I was sure," said Saul.

"You were sure?" Malynda tried to read Saul's face. Nothing there but glasses.

"Pisha Paysha," was all Saul replied. The man was reticent.

"You worked on this all by yourself?" Ezra had the promo on his screen now.

"All night. All by myself." Had the boys been out til New Year's like Malynda thought they would be, she would have said she spent the entire holiday working on it. Couldn't say that now.

"What do you think, Saul?" Ezra turned the screen in Saul's direction.

Saul looked up from his computer for the first time. He wheeled his chair a little closer to Ezra's desk and slid his glasses back up the bridge of his nose. Saul puckered his lips and blinked. "I love it," he said. "It's always been my favorite."

"Favorite?" Malynda thought. "He probably means style."

"It was the reason we hired Dan Oglesby in the first place," Ezra's eyebrows seem to point straight up as he turned back to Malynda.

"Can't forget a campaign like that," Saul wheeled back to his computer. "Classic." Saul was easy to read now. They both were.

Malynda had that look monsters get when the peasants are outside with the torches. "You know, you can't just fire someone in this state without paying them in full and Ruthie is out until after New Year's."

Both Saul and Ezra looked at each other then laughed as Ezra yanked a big grey envelope from his pencil tray and handed it to Malynda. "This is the Season of Miracles," he said.

Ezra looked down from the CEO office window as Malynda made trip after trip after trip, loading box after box after box of her framed certificates, diplomas and awards into the back of her car. Saul continued to pluck at his keyboard.

"I think she's finally done," Ezra said as he watched Malynda stumble around to her driver side door in the snow.

"How many boxes?" asked Saul.

"Six," answered Ezra.

"Shlemiel," said Saul.

"Dan Oglesby is a nice boy," said Ezra, watching her sedan pull away.

"He's a Mensch," said Saul.

"Probably will start his own company now," said Ezra.

"We always thought he would," said Saul.

"Just needed a nudge," said Ezra.

"She gave him a kick," said Saul.

"We should help him," said Ezra.

"His number's already on your desk," said Saul.

"Still playing that cockamamie game?" Ezra asked even though he could see it clearly on Saul's computer screen.

"Can't help it," said Saul. "The chickens shoot nuclear eggs out their tushies."

"Out their tushies?" repeated Ezra. Both men laughed.

Saul had been given the game by Johnetta Hoyle in hopes Hamelin Toys could figure out who designed it. Saul told her, one clever "yungotch" designed that code. "Whoever hires this person," Saul had said, "is going to make a fortune."

Ezra called Dan that very morning, wished his family a happy holiday, apologized for Malynda and told Dan he still had a job if he wanted it. Dan told Ezra about his plans for a website. To Dan's surprise, Ezra sounded absolutely delighted and offered to put him in contact with many smaller toy manufacturers that Hamelin Toys couldn't take on as clients because of inventory constraints. The brothers would even recommend him. When Dan asked Ezra why they would be so kind, Ezra said, "because there just aren't enough nice people in this business."

Saul had a list of toy companies with contact names, phone numbers and products delivered to Dan's house within forty-eight hours. He offered to send letters of introduction to any of them that Dan might be interested in.

That Christmas morning, Dan felt like God had smiled on him. Saul and Ezra felt like God had smiled on them. It wasn't long before a cottage industry of toy makers felt like God had smiled on them.

As for the kindly old man who had his bare bottom copied a zillion times at the office Christmas party in what became known around the break room as the Paper Moon Incident, he also got a call from Ezra. Zwang learned that, instead of being fired, he was now the new PM at Hamelin Toys. Zwang felt like God had smiled on him.

When the employees of Hamelin Toys learned that Malynda Piper was no longer their PM and that they were working for Zwang now, they felt like God had smiled on them. In fact, they threw the portly old Santa a surprise party to celebrate his big promotion. No copiers were involved.

In the end, everyone felt like God had smiled on them except Malynda Piper. Ironic since she got exactly what she wished for. She had no more worries about promos, car payments or rent for the simple reason she had no more job, no more car and no more apartment. Before next Christmas, Malynda Piper moved back in with her parents. Her parents didn't feel like God had smiled on them either.

Chapter 24:

The Cards on the Table

Not everyone has a stocking or a place to hang it. A two foot tall pre-decorated aluminum tree on his dining table and a small wreath of silver bells hung on the inside of his only front window was all the Christmas decorations Detective David Caldwell had. Not all that extravagant but plenty good enough.

He had three Christmas cards on his dining room table. One from his sister, one from his mother and one from Sarge. Sarge sent a card to everybody in the department. The grizzled old detective was crazy that way. The card from Caldwell's mother displayed an art deco nativity scene. The one from his sister showed a realistic Santa reading a letter surrounded by tiny elves. Sarge's was a pastoral of a snowman. But the sentiment scribbled on the inside of all three Christmas cards was the same: "For goodness sakes, David, find yourself a girl!"

David also had two presents: one from his sister; and one from his mother. The sister's present was definitely socks. The mother's was more cryptic. He hadn't opened either. David thought he would let them both simmer on the table a little while longer while he enjoyed his Christmas breakfast, a bowl of cold cereal and milk. It could have been better. The milk hadn't soured yet so it could have been worse. He even had enough juice for a full glass. A little Christmas miracle, he thought.

David clicked on his PC, also on the dining room table. Actually, everything was on his dining room table except the TV and it didn't work. He sent a simple message to the URL that cute quirky Oglesby girl had slipped him last night.

"Having a Merry Christmas?" he typed.

An instant later, came the response: "I am now!"

David smiled. So was he —now. The young detective could not know it but his life was about to become much better. The reason was in the cards.

Chapter 25:

Every One

There was a brief lull before the next round of noisy conviviality called breakfast. Darla and Dana —well, mostly Dana— had just finished bagging all the loose wrapping paper and ribbons scattered around the great room except for one long golden ribbon. Dana called Dawnet over and gave the long swirling ribbon to the little terrier. Since November, Dawnet had been drawn to that particular bow because it dared to be wide, golden and crackling. Today it would pay for that impertinence as Dawnet chewed, shook and wrestled it to shreds. There was not a Christmas squirrel in the Universe that could stand against his superior dogness. It turns out, one's discarded golden ribbon is another's Christmas squirrel.

Afterwards, Dana Oglesby balled up in one corner of the sofa, a huge pillow at her back, a fleece blanket tucked around her legs and dirty pink fuzzies. She was completely oblivious to the five wrapped gifts addressed to her and stacked neatly on the floor beside her or anything else as she typed away on her laptop between sporadic outbursts of giggles. The best presents always come unwrapped.

Debbie took what was surely her least expensive gift and ran to the phone to call Len Tobey, her best friend forever, to gush about it. Arnold Ogden Grubb Junior had dropped a present for her under the Oglesby Christmas tree during his little detour through their great room on Christmas Eve night. He had just bought it. As cheap as it was, it was all the jewelry Grubworm could afford —a lovely little Friendship bracelet of a wire form butterfly. Grampy Coy told her it was made of "Irish gold" because eventually it turned Debbie's wrist green. It wasn't the value of the bracelet so much as it was the meaning behind it. Whether Arnold Ogden Grubb Jr ever found himself or not, he cared enough to buy Debbie a present and spent every spare penny he had to do it. That one little piece of cheap jewelry did what his big brother's letter jacket could never do. The Grubworm was not a zero anymore. Caring is always cool.

Dotty had it tougher than her sisters. She kept bouncing from one toy to the next all morning, trying to determine which of the new batch would become her new favorite and which would be relegated to the collection neglected on her bedroom floor. It was very touch and go for awhile but her new Barbie seem to be winning out —like all her other Barbies before. There's comfort in familiarity.

Candy sat between the tree and that can of stale popcorn, cradling a purring Marmalade while admiring her new hairbrush. It was the prettiest hairbrush she had ever seen in her entire life. Once again, God had come through on another Christmas. This time with flying colors. She smiled broadly and imagined her mother using it to brush the tanglements out of her hair. Of course, that never happened. Wonderful so seldom happened to Candy. Except today. And Candice Siwel was thankful. It doesn't have to be big to be a blessing.

Stretched across Candy's legs and drifting off, Marmalade was content to finally have a calm, quiet soul who didn't move around much. The honey brown tabby was almost willing to overlook the annoying rambunctious play of that silly dog. Almost. Sometimes, a nice warm lap is all you ever need.

Darla and Dan were in the kitchen making their traditional Christmas breakfast: plate size pancakes with enough sweet toppings to put a hypoglycemic whale into a sugar coma along with scrambled eggs, of course, and a side of green and red peppers. Nothing says Christmas like green and red peppers. The only person who ate them was Grampy but it wasn't Christmas unless those peppers were on a serving dish somewhere. The whole family expected to see them. As always, breakfast would take a couple of hours to prepare what with Dan chasing Darla all around the kitchen. Darla didn't mind though. She loved the guy.

Grampy sat in his overstuffed Easy chair pretending to watch Bonanza. He listened to the antics in the kitchen, watched the youngest play with her toys, Little Dee chatter on the landline, Dawnet run himself into ecstatic exhaustion with that ribbon and Trouble there on the sofa thinking she was sneaking a few flirts in with her new boy friend. He was pretty sure Candy would become a permanent member of the family. Otherwise, that cat would be impossible to live with. The whole place was noisy, busy, messy and happy. The old man loved his family and loved being here. Just like the Christmas last year and the year before and the year before that. Every Christmas actually. Every one a blessing. Every one a miracle. Well, if you believe in miracles.

Skeptics will tell you all the consequences were foreseeable, the events inevitable, the coincidences circumstantial. No divine agency needed. Nothing to see here. Move along.

But who's going to believe a bunch of drunks? For no matter what skeptics tell you, miracles can happen and often do. Even on Christmas.

About the Author

Elmer Garten is a student of the human condition. Unfortunately, he flunked his final exam.

Made in the USA
Middletown, DE
23 September 2022

10928363R00149